A GIFT OF KINDLING
& OTHER STORIES

SNAPSHOT OF THE AUTHOR

PAT BECK

A GIFT
OF
KINDLING
&
OTHER
STORIES

THE MCCULLOUGH LIBRARY
North Bennington, Vermont
1978

Credits & Acknowledgments

ACKNOWLEDGMENTS: *Two of these stories, "A Promise in the Wind" and "Muskrat," first appeared in* Yankee *Magazine, with whose permission they are reprinted here.*

COVER DRAWING: *Pat Beck*

DESIGN: *William R. Scott*

TYPESETTING: *Hemmings Motor News, Bennington, Vermont*

PRINTING: *Excelsior Printing Co., North Adams, Massachusetts*

BINDING: *General Bookbinding Co., Inc., South Hadley , Massachusetts*

*Table
of
Contents*

"What really knocks me out is a book that, when you're done reading it, you wish the author that wrote it was a terrific friend of yours and could call him up on the phone whenever you like it...." (Holden Caulfield in J.D. Salinger's *Catcher in the Rye).*

The ten short stories in this collection make up such a book. Those of us who have read the voluminous manuscripts and notebooks of Pat Beck and chose these for publication were privileged to call her friend — as were and will be many of you when you read these stories now.

Patricia Beck was born April 8, 1924 in New York City's Hell's Kitchen, the daughter of a prominent figure in the sports world who died in 1928, and whose mother afterwards moved to Europe with her three children. Pat grew up in France, Spain and England. Her mother remarried, and World War II sent the family scurrying past German U-boats back to New Jersey.

She first came to Vermont in 1943 as a freshman at Bennington College. In 1948, after her mother's death, she purchased a home she named "Birdland" in North Bennington where she had already found many good friends and good relationships. She spent the rest of her life there except for the time, during her ten-year marriage to blind pianist Thomas Maulding, that she chauffeured him on his tours. Through the years her friendly charm and unstinting welcome drew young and old to that bird and animal sanctuary in North Bennington.

This slim volume is published by a few of her many friends as a tribute to Pat Beck, Vermonter by choice, human being, painter, author, who valiantly fought to make meaningful a life that tried to keep her down and at the end, true to her own spirit, made the final choice herself.

North Bennington, Vermont
November, 1978

Henry Christman
Margaret DeGray
Mary Delia Flory
Curtis Flory
Catherine Foster
Jane Hanks
Lucien Hanks
Ruth Levin
Frances Ross
William Scott

Four Lemons I

That winter had been a long hard struggle against blizzard-winds that piled drifts of snow chest-high to the horses pulling the sleighs. Even the skaters had deserted the lake. Though blasts of wind tore across the mirrored ice, there were a few men who huddled in their huts still hoping for their evening catch of pike.

Paul Spyro longed to break the monotony of dark blue mornings of snowfall and of nights that came early. His store was warm and well-lit and people were always stopping in for coffee or hot chocolate. The Gold B. maintained an atmosphere of open house for the town, it was not so much a place of business as it was a club whose membership was congenial and inexpensive. The fact of the matter was, one did not even have to purchase anything to go in and sit. Paul Spyro always seemed glad when his door opened and someone came in.

"How's the weather out there?" he would ask; and the conversation would start. Talk makes a man hungry, he knew, and soon a sandwich would be ordered, something to drink, something to smoke. Paul Spyro and his brother George made a living by working hard. They were open for the railroad crew at seven A.M. and closed around eleven P.M. In the summer they sold ice-cream which they made themselves and candy rolled out on a slab of marble that Paul Spyro had brought down from the top of Woodford Mountain years ago.

The back room smelled of cinnamon and ginger and butter and chocolate and the little coal stove was always red and hissing against the wind that rattled the windows. But that winter had been going on too long. It was already the beginning of March and not once had there been a thaw. The frost merely sank deeper into the earth and all over the town old-timers told of pipes that had never been frozen before, breaking. The snowcrews worked night after night to keep the tracks clear for the freights and the old Montreal-New York express that thundered through on its way north and south.

The men would come into the Gold B. to thaw themselves out and talk their talk of tracks and trains, of high and low "balls" — expressions which fascinated Paul Spyro, though he did not always understand what they were saying. The railroad men brought with them not only a sense of distance and time, but they gave Paul Spyro a dream. In the quiet hours, after the school-out rush of children to buy sweets and sodas, after the mill-out rush of men who got tobacco and ice-cream for supper, in these quiet hours the railroad men and their trains would fill him with a hunger, a restlessness. He longed to turn the key in the lock of the Gold B. and walk out under the maple-lined streets of the town, past the school and the churches to the freight houses where smoke-churning locomotives signaled and shunted all night causing light sleepers to turn in their beds at the constant activity. On the main line the signal light would switch from red to yellow to green, the train would disgorge rushing steam, bringing to life the metal thrusting arms which moved her wheels slowly at first, and in his hunger for newness he felt he could rush to board her moving off down the tracks which ran like silver rivers through the valleys and mountains of the land.

When this restlessness grew, he would take himself to the back room and make candy. Then George would take over the front of the store. Roasting the peanuts and melting the dark chunks of chocolate, or stuffing oily dates with walnuts rolled in sugar, Paul Spyro would find the wish to leave his store fade and soon he would carry out his tray of freshly made candies and place them in the glass case next to the tobacco and snuff.

But that winter had gone on for too long. The cold seemed to settle into his very bones, to weight his soul with its iciness; not even the candy-making could distract him. He was bored. So when the fat, fur-collared drummer came to this store and talked of games of chance and luck, an excitement began to take hold in him.

"Every third nickel is yours," said the drummer noticing this. "I have a machine out in the sleigh that's a great success. It's one of our best features. Why, in no time at all it will bring you in a whole new business. People like to take chances. And the pot grows bigger each day; they call it the *eagle.*"

They went out to the sleigh, and under an old bearskin rug the drummer showed him a machine of bronze etched with an eagle holding a streaming banner in his beak.

"Ain't she a beaut?" he said. He pulled the rug back further. Right below the claws of the eagle was a window in which colored slices of different fruits were stamped in metal on four rotating cylinders; a glass-lined container bubbled out at the bottom.

"Every third nickel goes into this pot. When the lucky turn comes—Zing! it opens and you have a very happy customer."

George came out beside them in the alley and peered into the sleigh. He saw the bronze eagle and the fruit gleaming in the window slot. Sensing the excitement in his brother, he frowned: he had never put any stock in Paul's unpredictable flyers in horses, in turkey-shoots, church lotteries and now that machine! But he saw the look on his brother's face and he knew his objections would make no difference at all in the matter.

The drummer took off his thick glasses and wiped them on his handkerchief, pausing a moment in his sales pitch. Because Paul Spyro had not objected but had followed him out to the sleigh, he was almost certain of his success; he smiled feeling pleased with himself.

"The eagle will net you a nice profit, and no work on your part. Fair's fair, I say — and someone's going to break the bank with four lemons and a jackpot. What do you say?"

Paul Spyro extended his hand. "You got yourself a deal."

The three men moved the heavy machine from the sleigh into the Gold B. The drummer took his order for the syrups and spices and other items for the store.

"I'll be back through in a month. Then we'll unlock the back. A third to a lucky customer, a third to me, and a third to you for doing nothing but watching people have the pleasure of betting on the pot." He turned up the fur-collar of his coat, "See you then," and stepped out to the sleigh. He flicked his whip and drove out of the alley onto the street. Paul Spyro listened to the sound of the bells and the muffled hoof beats going off in the distance.

The bronze eagle with the window showing slices of fruit had been placed next to the cash register and the door. When there were nickels in the change he made, Paul Spyro saw to it that they found their way to the slot. However, he also began to notice that his candy-case remained full. He was a good candy-maker and people had always come into the Gold B. for a bag of his home-made country sweets. "Gimme a bag of lemon drops, Paul," or "I'll take my change in caramels." Children left smudges on the glass case where they had pressed noses and fingers eyeing all the sweet things carefully before they purchased. He used to scold them sometimes, for they took so long and changed their minds so many times over their selections.

This past week the candy case had hardly been opened. Even children were putting their nickels in the machine. He decided to put the machine in the rear of the store. There were too many people coming in, too few sitting down to order something in the way of refreshment. Why, there were times when he didn't even know some of the men who walked to the rear to play the machine. Strangers bought packs of gum or cigarettes, to make change, and played the machine.

The sound of the nickels clinking down to the depths of the pot, the thump of the lever, the whirling rotation of the fruit in the window, and then the four sharp clicking stops began to make him nervous. Seldom did the little door open at the bottom. Frank Murphy was lucky, he got fifty cents. Sophie Green had started away when the machine spilled out a dollar's worth of nickels. All the time the round window at the bottom was filling up and showing the magnificent money growing from day to day.

He began to take a positive dislike to the bronze eagle that drew strangers and transients in increasing numbers, for it was robbing him of the quiet hours, of the daily exchanges with the people of his town. The door opened and closed so many times he didn't have a chance to ask how the weather was, or what was happening up the street. People no longer came in to sit and talk as before. They did not stop to buy a bag of his candy. The noise of the machine rang incessantly in his head.

Now and then a tempting trickle of money kept the promise bright. It was the third week. Any minute now...the turn of the wheel would come up; any minute the lucky nickel would turn up.

George was worried. He had not liked the idea of the machine in the first place. He was beginning to notice that when he went to make change he had to use pennies in place of nickels. Bill Powers at the bank had told him that he couldn't figure it, but they had run short of nickels, first time that had ever happened. The conductor of the trolley that ran across the valley to the next town had complained that people were riding short distances and asking for nickels in change. And soon the small talk and tales exchanged over the counter told of quarrels and fights. Henry Nash was not a drinker but he was five dollars short with his paycheck and his wife was blaming him for all sorts of indiscretions of which he was blameless. George knew that the money was locked in the bottom of the machine guarded by the sharpbeaked eagle.

And still the whip of winter snapped the air and the wind kept blowing as mournfully through the wires as the sound of the train whistle echoing through the valley at night. To the boredom born of that unending winter, Paul Spyro now felt the added tension created by that machine. In his experience of living, in his dealing with men and horses and machines, he knew something was wrong.

"Say Jake," he whispered, "how much you figure you're in for with the eagle?" Jake had put in about ten dollars over the three weeks.

One by one the brothers began questioning the men they knew had been playing the machine. Locking up one night they went in the back room and sat down together to add up the list. It was impressive in the amount the eagle had devoured, and meager in the times it opened its beak to pay off.

"Paul, what are we going to do? It must be fixed," said George.

He was thinking the same thing; only where there had been the excitement and the thrill of winning, now this cold reasoning with the facts made Paul realize that the machine was the set-up of a professional cheat. As far as he could see there was no gamble — the machine took and did not give back, and he was a part of this fraud.

"Help me drag it out back," he said to his brother. They went into the store and in the pale lemon light filtering in from the streetlight, slid the heavy machine into the back room.

"We better make sure," he said. With the small blade of his penknife he probed the lock on the back panel, twisted, turned and like a tiny key the knife opened the lock revealing a mechanism of clockwork behind the sections of fruit.

Paul Spyro put a nickel in the slot, pulled the lever and set the fruit whirling into position. One lemon, click; two lemons, click; three lemons, click; four lemons — slurred — bright red apple. He looked at George who said—

"It was almost the hundred-to-one shot."

"No," said Paul Spyro shaking his head, "you try."

George put a nickel in the slot, pulled the lever, one lemon,

click; two lemons, click; three lemons, click; four lemons —
slurred — peach.

Paul Spyro placed his finger on the wheel of the fourth slot
and rubbed. On the tooth of the gear was a tiny piece of metal so
that whenever the fourth lemon was about to fall into the slot,
the metal edged it over to another selection.

"I've been watching this performance all day trying to figure
out what went wrong. It's a wonder that no one spotted it before
we did. Must have been the excitement that kept them from
guessing."

"What do we do, Paul? The drummer is due any time. What do
we do? We cheated all those people out of their money."

Paul Spyro scratched his head. "If they get their money back
then they won't be cheated. Let's see how much there is here."

They counted one-hundred-eighty dollars worth of nickels.

"Now, we can figure from our list who spent what in the
playing."

The wind roared outside sending the snow whirling into
clouds of whiteness as they sat working out the sums on their
lists. They did not even hear the sleeper as she went through.
Finally it was finished.

"One little thing we do for Mr. Eagle," said Paul Spyro, "we
file his claws for him good." And he took a piece of wire twisting
it around one of the gears. He put the back panel on. He sat
down and on a piece of cardboard with a red crayon wrote OUT
OF ORDER. They slid the machine just outside the door. They
turned out the light in the back room and went upstairs to bed.

In the morning George mopped the tiles clean with hot water
and soap while his brother measured the water and soon the
Gold B. was filled with the fresh strong smell of the coffee. The
railroad men came in rubbing their hands and stamping their
boots. The tracks had been a cold place to have worked on a
night like that. Eggs frying and bacon and toast and now the
place had the old hum of talk and activity that gave it a quality all
its own.

Four

Lemons

"Say, Paul, what happened to that damn bronze eagle? What do you mean out of order?"

"Some kid comes in and jerks it too hard. The nickel drops and the wheels don't turn. How do I know what happened to the damn machine? What happens to any machine? Can't trust a one of them!. They all quit on you."

"I don't care what happens to *any* machine. I care about what happens to this one. I got seven bucks riding on that baby."

"Keep your shirt on," said Paul Spyro, "the guy who brought its due any day. He's got the key can open it. If he can fix it, you can play it."

"And what if he can't fix it? What about the pot then?" he protested.

"In that case you'll get back every damn nickel you put into her. You can take my word for that," said Paul Spyro. He looked up from the counter where he was furiously stabbing with a sponge an already immaculate marble-top. "Have you ever known when Paul Spyro wasn't as good as his word?"

The heavy winds abated and the snow seemed to fall gently, quietly, as if the whole town was settling down after the long winter to wait for the spring break.

Then, Paul Spyro recognized the sound of the drummer's horse and the sleighbells coming across the fields in the soft night hush. The store had been closed and he and his brother were in the back room having some cheese and wine. The town had settled in for the evening and the sound of the horse coming along the frozen ground rang loud and clear. The sleigh came to a stop in the alley behind the store. It took the drummer a minute to hitch his horse and throw a blanket over her. He stamped his boots and came in the back door. The heat from the coal stove threw a fog over his eyeglasses and he had to stop and take them off, wiping them against his overcoat.

"How's the weather out there?" asked Paul Spyro without looking up from his cheese and wine. He had stopped chomping the cheese and his jaw was set.

"Not so bad, but it's a long ride over Grafton any night," the drummer replied easily. "Got anything to warm a man's bones?"

Paul Spyro pushed the plate of cheese away from him and wiped the back of his hand across his mouth.

"What's the big idea of nearly getting us killed?" he said.

The drummer smiled, thinking this some kind of joke. "I don't know — you tell me."

Paul Spyro nodded to his brother and the two of them went into the store. The drummer heard the sound of something heavy being pushed and was surprised to see his machine shoved through the door with the out-of-order sign hung on it.

"What happened?" he asked. "I never knew these machines to go wrong." He took a key ring out of his pocket and went up to the machine and opened it. He noticed the wire at once. With his finger he felt where the ends were twisted together.

"Say, what are you guys giving me? What's this piece of wire doing here? What right did you have to open it?"

"A third for a lucky customer, a third for you, and a third for us?" asked Paul Spyro.

"Yeah, that's what I said, wasn't it?" The drummer was angry and felt the heat from the coal stove searing his face. "What's the matter with you guys?" He stood there with his hands on his hips, then he smiled, "or does fifty-fifty sound like better odds? You didn't have to do a thing but let the suckers play. Teach them not to gamble another time. What cause you fellers got to gripe? You got it made. You made a pile of loot on it."

"It's fixed," said George quickly.

"So?" said the drummer. He looked at George and Paul Spyro, at the indignation on their faces. Then he tapped his finger on the side of his head; a smile breaking the tenseness of his question. "Hey — hold the phone, Mac, I'm getting the picture now. You guys," and now he started to laugh, "you guys believed it would pay off legal! You believed there was a real hundred-to-one shot. Brother, this is good."

Instead of answering, Paul Spyro walked over to the woodpile in the corner and reached down for an axe.

The drummer had stopped laughing. His face was white.

Four Lemons

There were beads of sweat forming on his upper lips. "What are you going to do with that axe?" he asked hoarsely.

George watched his brother raise the axe shoulder high and swing the blunt end against the metal machine, opening a dent halfway down the side. The money hurled like bullets inside. He swung again, his face reflecting his rage. The back panel was shorn off its hinges and fell with a crash. The third time he swung the axe, the bronze eagle was ripped open from his wings diagonally down across his chest to his claws; a mess of nickels poured from the wound.

The drummer was standing there trembling at the sight of the anger of the man with the axe. He began to talk fast, wiping his upper lip with his coat sleeve. "All right," he said, "keep it. I don't care what you do with it. Only put away that Goddamn axe."

But Paul Spyro seemed almost not to have heard. "For years I work with these hands," he said deliberately, "I melt my own chocolate, I buy the best walnuts I can find, make my own candy with imported spices, and real butter. I work long hours, hard hours. No machine punk is going to come along and cheat people in my store." He stopped and the sound of his lungs breathing in air was loud. "Get this pile of junk out of here," he said pointing to the broken bronze eagle. "The cops asked me where I got it, but I told them I forgot, but if you know what's good for you..." He didn't finish, he gripped the handle of the axe till his knuckles were white with strain.

George helped the drummer load the broken eagle onto the sleigh and cover it with the old bearskin rug. They saw him stuff pieces of straw in the sleighbells to muffle the sound, as if the ringing of them in the night would call down his guilt upon him for all to see. Then they heard the sound of the horse's hooves chomping fainter in the distance.

Afterward, Paul Spyro went for the broom and dustpan to sweep the money up off the floor. "Tomorrow morning we pay off," he told his brother, while the coins clattered into the pan, "tomorrow everyone gets four lemons. We'll tell them the damn eagle broke."

What about the money that's left over? What about the names we haven't got on our list?" said George. "What happens to the other third?"

Paul Spyro sat down and reached for the wine-bottle. He poured two glasses of wine and passed one to his brother. Then he said, "Well, what about it? A man's got a right to a small profit. It's a fair gamble, ain't it? Fair's fair, like the man said....Tell you what. We'll get some of that fancy cinnamon and ginger for our next batch." He took a drink of wine and winked at his brother. "It all goes back into the business, anyway. A man's got a right to a small profit, I say, and no harm done."

George savored his wine, smiling. "Tell you what, Paul — suppose I make a batch of spearmint patties in the morning. Need something green to hurry the spring. This winter has gone on long enough." When they finished their drinks, they turned off the light, and went upstairs to bed.

Four
Lemons

One of the Green Mountain Boys II

The springs of the bed twanged as Allan turned on his back. With his toes he touched the bottom rung. He thought how big that bed used to feel in his grandfather's house. A rooster crowed from some farm. He was conscious of the blanket he had drawn about his body. August nights could be cool in Vermont. Every other year, since the divorce, he took a jet from Los Angeles to New York where he would visit his father and during this time he would come north also to this small red frame house on the edge of the woods. It was an old and comfortable house, with a colored afghan thrown over the sofa in the living room and portraits of past generations of Mattesons and other relations on the walls. Outside, Grandma's flower and vegetable garden stretched to the fringe of sugar maples. Since her death four years ago, Gramps had put special care into tending the needs of the garden. Bird houses, like sentry boxes, bordered the limits where the goldenrod had taken over. It was here one misty morning that his father, when he was a young boy, had poked the stuffed deer head slowly above the weeds knowing the old man's habit of checking for what wildlife moved near the woods. "I began counting to see how long it would take him," Allan remembered his father's story, "and at the count of nineteen that shotgun blasted away. It rained fur, and horns, and goldenrod." Allan chuckled to himself in bed as he imagined how excited

Gramps must have felt with his shots going true to target. Gramps had also seen his son's hasty departure through the meadow mists and had heard the boy's laughter. "I ate my supper cold and standing," his dad had concluded, "never again did I go rooting in the attic for any more trophies for my father to shoot up."

Allan sniffed buttermilk pancakes, sausages, the smell of coffee floated up the stairwell. He glanced at his wristwatch, quarter to seven, but though he stayed as long as he could in bed when home, he found himself dressing hurriedly here and going downstairs to wash.

"Morning, Gramps," he said as he passed the kitchen. The tall man in a green checkered shirt with a white apron around his wide girth tipped his spatula.

"Thought these would get you up. For a quarterback you're darn skinny. How many yards you say you ran on that touchdown pass?" He flipped the sausages to brown on the other side.

"Forty-eight yards," Allan smiled, "in the last five seconds of the game. Won the championship too. If I play as well as a senior, I can get a football scholarship."

"Six feet tall but don't weigh no more than a hummingbird," Gramps sniffed.

"O.K.," Allan grinned, "after I wash I'll eat a stack of those cakes swamped in maple syrup, and ten sausages."

A bark from the back porch announced the arrival of Ethan who also found the smells to his liking. Allan opened the screen door for the beagle who rushed to him for attention. He had seen the pup grow into a dog, now heavy in body, with gray whiskers along his nose and chin.

"Gramps," Alan thought back to that early joke with the deer trophy, "what did Ethan do when your prize head was shot?"

His grandfather turned from the sizzling skillet to face him. For a second his brow was drawn in anger but then he broke into a deep laugh. "He done what any good hunting pup does, retrieved me what was left of an antler. To think that I had hiked way over Glastenbury Mountain for that buck, and I almost couldn't shoot him when I saw him standing on that ridge."

Having heard his name, sensing that he was part of the conversation, Ethan rubbed up against his owner. "Yup, you were a good hunter, weren't you?" He bent to scratch the dog's back and Ethan barked. "I know you want some of these cakes too but you got to wait your turn same as the rest of us."

"Won't be long washing," Allan said going into the bathroom. He combed his brown hair worn forward and medium long as was the style at Muir High. He searched in the mirror for some of the Matteson features. They were there, the broad forehead, deep-set blue eyes and the almost square chin. A Matteson had died at The Battle of Bennington. One summer Gramps and he had charted their own map from the locations on the bronze marker at the top of the battlefield to track down as best they could the place where he had probably fought. The land looked as though it had not changed since that time. It was different from the box type houses in the valley in California where he had to commute by bus to a central high school. "Gramps," he shouted, "I'll always be a Vermonter, won't I?"

The curtains that Grandma had made still hung over the kitchen sink but the blue gentians on them had faded. A neighbor woman helped keep the house neat by coming to clean three times a week.

"Gramps, it never seems to change here," Allan said, biting into a forkful of golden cakes. Some butter and syrup ran down his chin but he licked it off before it fell.

Gramps stirred the sugar in his coffee and studied the boy. Lines of sadness creased his face as he replied, "Don't seem the same to me without Nattie."

After eating two helpings, Allan left some sausage and cake on his plate which he placed on the floor beside him. It was the family tradition. "Ethan's going to do the dishes," and he laughed seeing the swift pink tongue wipe the plate clean.

"Better go dig us some worms if we plan on trying out your present, Gramps." Allan watched the deep blue eyes return from the past. He finished his coffee and went over to the long cylinder his grandson had brought him the night before. Carefully he took out the glass rod and ran his fingers along it. "Say you bought this yourself?"

"I pumped gas, changed tires, washed cars every chance I could get. It's a good one, isn't it?"

"A lollapalooza," Gramps said. Allan laughed at his old-fashioned expression.

"Come on, Ethan, we'll go dig the worms." Allan carried his plate over to the sink where he ran cold water on it. He walked out to the back porch and stretched. This year, as always, the wire for the green vine which would burst with blue rockets of morning-glories was tied to the roof. A streak of ginger shot past the shed sent the beagle scampering down the steps in pursuit of a hunting cat. The baying dog reminded him of all the hunting tales his Dad and Gramps used to tell. From the shed, Allan took a spade and an old coffee can, walked to the woods where he would only have to lift stones to find the worms. A puffball deflated under his sneaker. This must have been a summer with rain.

The towers of the Thaxton mansion could be seen over the tree tops. When it had been an estate, his grandfather had been in charge of the lawns and gardens. "We grew everything from melons to prize-winning roses. Nattie won blue ribbons for her pickles at the state fair. I wish you could have seen the oriental fruit garden in bloom. Mr. Thaxter had it enclosed by the brick wall to keep out the foxes and the children who came after the fruit. The bee hives were there also."

When his parents had separated it had shaken him deeply to be moved to California. Then he had tried not to remember how happy they had been as a family. But with Gramps, all the many details of what had been joy continued to live within him. He looked from the sturdy brick wall to the path worn through the woods by countless people who used it as a short-cut to the village.

When he was only a little fellow, he had followed it once to the house of an old lady. "What you want, sonny?" her eyes had squinted at him through the screen door. "Mama says an old witch lives in the woods and I want to see what an old witch looks like." How she had laughed, throwing her head back to reveal but three teeth. She had said that she reckoned he had to be Matt Matteson's boy what with that innocent face asking such a fool question. He had been invited in for a glass of cool milk and cookies which she had just taken out of the oven. It was here that his mother had found, his stomach bulging from all the old woman had fed him. "Don't think it right to scare a young'un by telling him a witch lives in the woods," she had told his mother. "Still folks from the east ain't got much manners. Matt would have done better marrying Sally Bridges instead of a Boston female."

When she had gotten him home, his mother had spanked him for wandering off but she realized it had been partly her doing. He had then been held and kissed. She had told him that the old lady's name was Miss Katherine Sparks and some afternoon she would make a pot of beans and they would go pay her a call. She had laughed when he had said that he thought the old witch was very nice. "Katherine Sparks, Miss Sparks," his mother had reminded him. "Mama, she knew I was a Matteson, knew that I belonged to Dad."

Allan figured that he had enough worms so he put the can down, covered it with ferns and went into the woods until he came around the hill leading to the Sparks' house. where her garden had been, he saw the harvest of rocks from the bulldozer's plow, complete as the devastation in war. Gramps had written him that the house had been sold two months after Miss Katherine's death to a young couple working at the clinic. Allan saw the foundation for their swimming pool. Not even her favorite plum tree had been spared; a lone hollyhock grew by the back door. Sadly he turned away from where he had spent many good times of his childhood. As he left the woods, he felt the sun warm on his body.

"Yup, that should do it," Gramps said as he looked into the

can with not quite enough soil to cover the wriggling warms. "Pour a little water on them. We want them fresh and tasty for Mr. Trout."

The breakfast dishes had been washed and were draining while he had been outside, and in their place on the table were the things his grandfather had collected for their trip. "Guess you can use Old Ben," he nodded to his bamboo rod. "No sense of letting it go to waste now that I got me this humdinger."

Allan laughed, "Gramps, where do you get all those crazy words? I'll bet the kids at Muir High wouldn't dig you."

"Why, am I some kind of worm that I must be dug?" his grandfather scowled but seeing how Allan was smiling, he smiled too. "You are referring to the generation gap. It don't bother us none, does it?"

"No sir, it sure as heck don't," Allan replied.

"You got that same spirit of deviltry your father had when he was a young'un. Let's go and don't forget we've got to stop for your fishing license."

The tractor was still parked in the garage next to the Ford. Allan remembered when it had been bright red and shinning. This mud-covered machine seemed smaller. Apparently after Gramps retired no one took much care of it.

"When you used to scare us all to death by wandering off," Gramps said, "ten to one I'd find you sitting up there on the saddle. Don't know how you managed never to fall off 'cause I've seen you when you were sound asleep with your eyes open."

"I wasn't asleep," Allan answered, "I used to be plowing the west pasture, or bringing in the hay wagons. I did all the things you did, Gramps, but in my mind while I was sitting up there. That's how come I never tumbled."

"You don't take after your pa in that respect. All he was ever interested in was going fast, on his bike, later on his motorcycles."

In the small bedroom where Allan slept, which had been his father's, were the framed snapshots of a racing bike, then various motorcycles, and a portrait of a handsome young man with the wings of the Air Force on his tunic.

They got into the car and drove down the hill into the village. Allan went in to the post office with his grandfather. Usually more news was to be gathered here than in the evening paper, but today there was only a young mother herding three children out the door, her arms laden with catalogues and magazines. Gramps peeked into his box and then turned to leave.

The park was across the street. In the bright sunshine, Allan saw that the World War II roll call had been replaced by a granite marker dedicated TO ALL VETERANS. In the past visits he had always gone over to find with pride his father's name. Vandals had stoned the old glass-covered board and it was gone.

Then he looked at the railroad station adjacent to the park. From the handsome building shown in the family photograph album, it had fallen into a neglected wreck. Pigeons wheeled like clouds about the mansard roof. The tracks were no longer as ribbons of silver through the valleys as the passenger trains were no longer in service. Occasionally a Diesel engine shunted on the spur leading from the factory to its furniture warehouses.

"Sad to see her sitting there like an old neglected lady," Gramps said, seeing where the boy was looking. "Once you could get a ticket at that station to go north to Montreal, or south to New York City." He put his callused hand to his chin. "Why Admiral Dewey himself came here to speak from the observation car. He wore a white cap and a chest full of medals that caught the sun like small stars when he moved. And after the war, President Wilson stopped. All us boys lined up in uniform and he came down to shake our hands. I told him I never got overseas, never left New Jersey, but he shook my hand just the same, 'you were a doughboy and the country is grateful.' A flu epidemic had struck the camp where I had been stationed. Me and a couple of others were on burial duty. We used to carry the corpses out of the tents."

"That's when you took to chewing tobacco, wasn't it, Gramps?" Allan could have continued any one of his grandfather's numerous tales. He loved to hear them over again the same way he had loved to hear his mother reading aloud, "Treasure Island", or, "The Tale Of Two Cities".

Gramp's blue eyes looked deep into his own. "Do you remember everything I tell you?"

"First time I saw you chew," Allan beamed, "I thought you had the mumps because your jaw was so swollen. But your buddy had told you that the tobacco plug would keep you from catching flu."

"Right he was too, so I don't suppose it was a mistake, I mean about the president shaking my hand, 'cause I might not have survived if I hadn't known about chewing tobacco." He turned his back on the station and got into the car. "Next stop the county clerk's."

Telling the woman behind the desk that his birthplace had been Vermont gave Allan a twinge of pleasure. The small office, its walls lined with topographic maps was his land, his birthright. He slipped the license in the plastic folder and pinned it to the faded blue sailing cap he wore.

"Thought we'd try the Battenkill before it gets too crowded. After lunch we'll head for Sunderland," Gramps said, steering the car over another section of tracks and onto Rt. 7. "We'll just take it slow and easy," but he pressed his foot on the accelerator.

"Guess I know from what side of the family Dad got his love for speed," Allan teased as they passed a gravel truck lumbering along.

'Not breaking any law," Gramps replied, "he gave me the go-ahead. I'm doing fifty and we got us some fishing to do."

There were two cars parked at the cut by the river with no one in sight, so Gramps pulled in. They exchanged boots for shoes and went through the process of stringing the lines on their rods, attaching leaders to their hooks, selecting what weights to use.

"Now for a tasty worm," Gramps said, hooking one on just so.

"A day like today they should go for worms." He stood on the bank, squared his feet, shuffled them in the dirt where countless fishermen before had worn the place smooth as a back lot homeplate. He flicked his wrist several times. "Yup, a lollapalooza," and he cast his rod over his shoulder, the line went singing out to the middle of the river. The current took it, drew the slender tip down where it tightened and danced above the water.

"Great cast," Allan said. He felt a tightness in his stomach as he tried to place his line to the inside. It landed close to the white water splashing against stones. He began to reel in.

"No, no, leave it there. Trout often lie in the shadows of stones. Keep your fingers on that line, though, for with this high current a trout's first nip might go unnoticed."

Gramps sat on a piece of planking left on the bank. Allan was too excited to sit. His fingers felt the pulling of the water and the dancing tip had him hypnotized. Even though they were on the shady side of the river the sun's glare tired his eyes. He knew it also made it hard for the trout to see him. During the first hour Gramps had reeled in two rainbows.

"Kind of a skimpy lunch. Let's try out luck at Minister's Hole."

Every dip and turn in the river had a name and Allan knew this one to be not far down opposite a house which had once belonged to a minister. Allan reeled in, securing the hook to the corked handle. They gathered their equipment, returned to the highway to walk about a quarter of a mile west, then they cut across a field of clover.

"Notice what's been living in the hedges?" Gramps asked.

A trail of bent grass led to the thicket. Allan saw the droppings of deer. The sweet grasses and flowing water provided them their needs; high ground leading to the mountains on each side of the river was their sanctuary. They must have been on the higher elevations now for he could spot none.

At another worn place on the bank they cast into slower

moving water as here the river broadened, ran shallow. They used lighter weights. The trees above them offered some protection from the sun although it was getting hot. Allan opened his shirt at the neck.

"Al..." his grandfather whispered as he stared at the bamboo tip. Again it dipped slightly.

Allan tightened his hold and on the third nip he jerked the line. "Got him," he cried, reeling in as the trout broke water.

"Easy, play him easy if he's going to fight."

The pole bent as Allan struggled to get the fish in the net without losing him.

"Now that's what I call a trout," his grandfather said as he watched Allan retrieve the hook from the gills, then break the neck as he had taught him. "You get him cleaned while I act as chef." He began collecting stones to contain the fire.

By late afternoon they had fished three other holes without success. "We'll try one more before we quit," Gramps said.

The seat of the car felt soft to Allan who leaned back feeling tired. "Hope some of the energy of this land wears off on me," he sighed, "or is it inherited by birth?"

"What's going to happen to you when they get you in the army?"

His grandfather caught him by surprise for though they often watched the news on TV they had never discussed the war. "Maybe you're one of those boys who might find Canada a good place for a long vacation?"

"You should know me better than that, Gramps," Allan replied. In fact he felt the anger rising as fire within him. "I'm going to college. I need all the education I can get to survive in this world. Dad said if I applied to some place in the East he'd have more time to be with me and I talked it over with Mom. I want to go to the University of Vermont. As for Vietnam," he lowered his voice, "I don't believe we should be there. If they draft me of course I'll serve. But it isn't like your war, or Dad's." He looked at how his grandfather betrayed nothing but concentration on his driving. "Gramps," he paused, "I thought you knew me better than that."

His grandfather reached his large hand over and scratched Allan's head. "You're a Matteson, boy. Don't get riled up 'cause you run out of steam. Now I'm going to take you to a place you haven't been."

They crossed back over the tracks onto the Main Street of the village. Gramps turned in past the gatehouse of what had been the Thaxter estate. "View Of The Mountain Clinic" the sign read. Then he turned off past the mansion to a dirt road.

"Where are we going, Gramps?" Pot holes caused the car to buck. "Is this the old quarry road?"

"Yup. Sage Creek runs through the quarry and empties into a pond but just before it does there is one heck of a deep hole."

Branches swept across the windshield and Allan pulled his arm off the window rest. "You catch trout there?"

"Nope. We're after what folks around here can't seem to catch but I got me a hunch that the two of us can." He turned to Allan, "pike."

"You mean those long fish that look like submarines? I went in to say hi to Mike, the barber, who was talking to Doc Harris. He told how no one knew how to lure them." Allan rubbed his jaw. "I don't know, Gramps, if Mike Bouplon couldn't catch one..."

"Say what he used for bait?"

"Bought one of those hinged contraptions that looks like a bug."

His grandfather grunted with satisfaction. He turned the car onto a sand cutaway and got out. "Figure we'll go along the ridge and look down on them. Harder work than where Bouplon fishes." He pulled a red bandana out of his creel and unfolded an oval of blue steel with a hooked claw underneath. "Fashioned it myself. In the water it's going to look real." Allan knew this was something special. He left his gear in the car and they began the steep climb to the top of the quarry.

It was that quiet time, the hush before twilight when

everything was still. Only the pebbles rolling down from where they had stepped made any noise. The quarry had not been mined for over sixty years although the trail was still open. Around it was an overgrowth of bushes and trees. Now the old man was grunting from exertion. They were almost at the top. Shielded from what warmth the sun had given, Allan felt a chill spring along his arms where the hairs stood up in the dampness. A mourning dove whistled plaintively from a thicket. The shadows were lengthening as they reached the summit. His grandfather lay on his stomach and crawled to the edge, waved the boy over. "Yup, there they are," he whispered.

Allan inched over taking care not to send a pebble falling. Then he saw them too, the long dark bodies, four of them anchored like subs in the deep gray water. The trees around them were cutting off what light was left. "Gramps, it'll be getting dark soon."

"Sh," the old man cautioned, "I got me a flashlight. Now I'm going to let a little blue bug dance in front of the pack. Easy, little blue," and he inched the line over the side of the lichen growing on the rock. When it hit the water the lure spun to life like a hungry bug searching for a meal. The pike remained stationary. The cry of a rabbit coming through the underbrush startled Allan momentarily. Gramps was frozen in concentration. He moved the line in front of the four, then swung it away from them. Suddenly a small pike appeared and lunged, its voracious jaws opening and closing over the lure. Gramps pulled sharply. "Got him!" and he began hauling him up the side of the quarry. It was almost dark now, but from its weight he knew it was not one of the large pike.

Later, Allan had tried to reconstruct just what it was he saw and heard after that long scream had stopped his breathing. The strange flurry of wind touched his face and his grandfather roared with fury. There was the clatter of stones falling from where they lay and the dark shadow rising with the flailing fish. The rod was pulled off the ledge. The darkness hid what it was that had swooped down on them. The stillness returned after the shrieking echoes had died out in the quarry. Black water hid the pike. Above the trees the sky was blue-gray.

Gramps made his way down the trail with Allan by using the flashlight. The extra patch of light when the car door was opened comforted Allan.

"Gramps, what happened?"

"They won't believe me," he said, wiping his brow with the bandana. "I doubt if you would either unless you'd been there."

"Believe what?" Allan was still puzzled as to what happened. "You mean about dropping your rod?"

"I didn't drop my rod, boy. Didn't you hear him attacking?"

It had taken place so swiftly that Allan was still not sure of what he had hard or seen — the shrieking, the fury of a sudden wind.

"The fish hawk, Allan," his grandfather stated. "That osprey made a beeline for my pike. Sunk his claws in tight, pulled the whole dang rod and reel to boot out of my hands. My brand new rod you worked so hard to get me. And damn if they go and draft you. How are we ever going to fish again, boy?"

This sudden collapse worried Allan. He put his arm on his grandfather's shoulder. "Heck, if I go to college in Burlington, I'd be coming up weekends to see you. And there's nothing to keep you from driving up to watch me catch fabulous passes."

By the car light he saw that his grandfather had not lost his fear. "You have something all your life," he spoke softly, "then suddenly its taken from you. Why, Nattie wasn't sick a day in her life." Wearily he pulled his boots off.

"Wait till you tell Doc and Mike Bouplon this tale," Allan tried to break his mood, "proably be good for a free haircut."

He tried to joke the man out of his despair, but the dark quarry had held in its shadows a swift moving prey and the talisman of being safe with family, safe with the bonds of memory and love, carried no weight. A man was on his own. "Gramps," he tugged at his sleeve, "Dad told me to treat us to a couple of steaks some night, and if you're as hungry as I am..."

"A damned osprey," his grandfather growled, "and he got

away with my pike, small as he was, and my brand new rod." He stood up and shook his first at the quarry. "I'm coming back in daylight and see if I can't find me that rod dangling from some tree. Just as I had me a pike. You saw that I had him, didn't you, Al?"

"Yup, Gramps, Let's go eat." As he sat next to his grandfather he thought of the whirlwind nature of the fish hawk's attack, the ferocious jaws of the pike snapping shut on the metal lure, and how one day, in some far off country he might be taken by surprise again no matter how much he had been taught, how much he had remembered, for a man is always on his own.

"Blamed osprey," his grandfather chuckled and Allan knew that a man coming from this state should have something of the quality of endurance from its granite, the spirit of the Mattesons, passed from father to son, even though they had fought, and one had died at the Battle of Bennington. "Yup, Gramps," he yawned, "that pike wasn't much, but man, was that fish hawk a lollapalooza?"

Age of Reason III

Kate Ahearn had disobediently climbed to the top of the big hill with her sled. From this height the icy run twisted and turned, losing itself in the bottom thickets. The girl in front shot off on her sled with the striped scarf flying in the wind. "Go on, you're holding us all back." Kate was given a shove. She hesitated for she had only come to look; the lower grades were not allowed to use this hill. Then Sister Veronica, standing on the crest like a big ruffled bird, made a sweeping gesture, her open mouth, a scream in the November wind. Prodded and shouted at by the others, Kate took three running steps, threw herself on the sled. It bucked, swept down the glaze. Below, figures in black uniforms were struggling their way up the sides. Carefully she held the sled to the middle of the run. The cold wind tore at her face and blinded her eyes. The runners tore over the ice gaining momentum. Someone shrieked as she passed. Her fingers grasped tighter on the sled. Such steepness took away her breath. In the fierce wind, suddenly the jolting stopped — the screech of metal runners stopped. As she was flung off, she heard, very clearly a voice cry, "The child has killed herself." She was knotted by a twist of pain.

"In goes the good air," hands pressured on her back, "Out goes the bad air," as someone administered artificial respiration. Gradually her breathing commenced and she turned to see Sister

Mary, her worried face tighten into anger. "You could have killed yourself, Kate Ahearn," she said. "And look at your uniform. You've ripped the cuffs off."

It was true, the celluloid cuffs were gone. She was surprised to see that her wrists were bleeding. The bright drops fell on the snow, and then she began to cry.

"Come along, come along to the infirmary to see what else you've done to yourself, though it's no one's fault but your own. The younger group has had specific rules against using that hill," Sister Mary scolded.

The iodine stung, but the cool white bandages on her wrists made her feel better. "Thank the Lord, no bones are broken. Just a good old-fashioned belly-whopper is what you had," the nun said. "Oh, but you're a wild one," and Kate lowered her eyes against the fimiliar tirade against what had come to be called her "wild Irish blood". In the silence each movement of the woman in the black rustling habit filled Kate with dread. Nameless her fear hid underneath. She sat up straighter. "And not a bit repentant, are you?" the nun said.

"I'm sorry," Kate bowed her head, "It went so fast I couldn't steer anymore."

"That's not what I meant. You shouldn't have climbed up there in the first place." The nun put the gauze and iodine in a cabinet and locked it. "Go along with you. Scat, and instead of running around like that, go to the store for another pair of cuffs. You're a disgrace."

Kate's knees were not up to running. "Yes, Sister." At least she had not been given a punishment. Then she remembered that would probably come when Father William was getting her ready for confession. The thought of giving up fifteen cents out of her quarter allowance for the cuffs was the sorrowful part of the whole adventure.

In the store, she moved past the penny candy without a look, to the rear where soaps, notions and the dry goods were kept. A row of silver crucifixes marked the boundary between the secular and the religious articles. A cloth heart stamped with a crown whose thorns were tipped with red caught her eye. Lots of the girls wore scapulars around their necks on a ribbon, or pinned to their slips or pajamas. Maybe if she wore one she would then not always be getting into trouble. Next week perhaps. The new cuffs covered the bandages, their stiffness pressured her wrists which began to throb.

To make matters worse, this was the day green gage plums were served for lunch. "Ginger," she whispered, "Do me a favor and eat my plums?"

Ginger O'Connell had a birthday in October also making her eight and had the cubicle next to hers in the dormitory. She was noted for her ability to consume just about everything that was served at the long wooden table. "Boy, Kate, someday you're going to get it good. I heard about the accident this morning. Is it true that you're scarred for life?" She opened her mouth and plopped in one of the plums which caused Kate to look away. She could not bear their thick pulpy skins.

Ginger had noticed the disgust. "Swallow them whole, like communion. That way they're not so bad," and she licked the juice off her upper lip.

"Here," said Kate, "You like them. Take mine."

"Can't," persisted Ginger. "I already ate Clara's and Dodo's. Besides you don't have to eat them. Use your system."

The system was Kate's idea. It simply meant concealing the disliked item of food in a napkin, then getting permission to go into the pantry for a utensil, dumping the paper in the trash can. There was a small element of risk, but this never bothered her so she brought the napkin to her lips as if wiping her mouth, and one by one she cleaned the fruit from her bowl. She hoped the paper would not split as the syrup began seeping through. With permission, she carried it to the pantry and deposited it in the can just before one of the monitors came in with a sugar bowl. Quickly Kate took a spoon out of the drawer. "I dropped mine," she smiled as a bell rang for the children to file out of the dining hall.

In the library, for the first time that day, Kate had a chance to think about what had happened. Ever since Sister Veronica had signaled her down the hill she felt as though she were still falling through space. The doubt of not knowing who to believe had begun when she had been placed in the convent three months earlier. The sister who had told her not to climb the hill, and the one who had told her to go ahead, actually had left the decision up to her. Was the accident a punishment for this choice? Sister Mary had implied that in the infirmary, yet she knew that she must confess her disobedience before the priest. It was the cold wind in her eyes which had caused her to hit the half-buried tree on the side of the run. Perhaps she should pray in the chapel at the Stations of the Cross, wear a scapular with its heart of bloody thorns instead of thinking how her own wrists had been cut in the morning? She wished that her parents had placed her in a regular school. There were so many rules to follow here; the bells rang constantly for each routine to start; all these women in black — eat this, drink that, confess and pray, don't read that, read this; and still with the spirit of rebellion born against the dread of her wildness of blood, she dragged her chair over to the bookcase to take down the biggest book she could find from the seventh grade selections. As it was, the place seemed deserted, the act unobserved. Carefully she carried it over to one of the tables by the window, opened it to an illustration which at once fascinated her. A naked man with a flowing cloth about his thighs was chained by his wrists to a rock, while above him, circled a huge bird, its claws outstretched in attack. The man's face was angry, his body helplessly awaiting the cruel talons. What had he done, she wondered, that he was chained to this lonely rock? Who could have done such a thing to him? His arms pinned back made her think of that other man, the one on the cross with his head bowed. Staring at the picture, she began to see the bird was circling closer, closer to his body, when a shadow spread over the rock.

"Merciful Heavens, child, you'll ruin your eyesight poring over a book that way." And she heard the dry rustling sound such as leaves make being blown in the woods as Sister Veronica approached. Kate closed the pages. "What is it that fascinates you so?" asked the nun, taking the book in both hands to hold closer to her spectacles. "Greek mythology? Katherine Ahearn," the gray eyes behind the glass pinned her down, "You know you are to take books from your section only. Why is it you persist in breaking every rule you can find?"

And remembering how the nun had summoned her forward that very morning, Kate said, "But it was you who told me to come ahead. You swept your arm forward."

For a moment only the nun's face betrayed an emptiness of expression until the brows contracted and her voice was angrily explaining how she had not known whom she had summoned to go, and what on earth did that have to do with reading the wrong book, that a child such as she was made for more trouble than all the others, and here Kate got lost hearing about ninety-nine sheep as opposed to the one who strayed. Sister Veronica changed the tone of her words. "I'll put the book back for you and we'll say nothing further. Besides, isn't it about time for your instruction with Father William?" Reaching out, her fingers lightly touched the black serge uniform, and Kate felt her wrists ache under the bandage.

Father William's study was at the other wing of the main building and Kate walked down the long dark halls always so empty and cold. When no one answered her knocking, she entered as the priest had told her to do. A shaft of sunshine lit the rose-flowered carpet running the length of the room and the cold breeze from an open window had wiped away that fine dust which she imagined the rustling habit's of the nuns scattered in their paths. Somehow even the holy water she used to bless herself contained the lifeless scent from their fingers. His room was not like the rest of the school, she thought, taking pleasure from the bird plates along the walls. She climbed upon the green leather couch where it was her custom to sit during these visits. The smell of his pipe tobacco lingered here with a trace of the fields from his Gordon setter, "Mac". Typical of the man's kindness, he had left an open box of wafers for her visit. She reached over, popped one into her mouth. Her teeth, her tongue searched for sweetness yet the curious fact was it was as if she were eating air. Each one she tried tasted the same. Out of politeness, the last three she did not consume.

"Holy Mother of God," he bellowed when he came in, "The child has eaten the communion wafers." His soft white hand struck his forehead, a severe gesture were it not that Kate saw the grin which he then quickly concealed. She was sorry she explained, but he had always before given her a treat.

"After your instruction, Kate, after," he said, sinking into the armchair opposite. "In a manner of speaking I did leave the wafers out for you. As you may recall this was to be your first lesson in how to receive communion, and what it is that you're receiving."

"Father?" she asked, "why is it they tasted like air, like nothing?"

Helplessly the priest brough both palms down sharply on his thighs. "Kate," he struggled for some control of his voice, "I'm sure all those foreign schools your parents thought so fine for you have done irreparable damage. You should have received communion, for instance, at seven, when you had reached the age of reason. Why it is that you alone in your grade have to be given instruction on how to receive the Blessed Host."

"I'm sorry," she repeated for the second time that day feeling how matters got worse without her knowing quite why.

Then Father William straightened himself in his chair. "Well, we might as well begin. You had the foresight to leave three wafers and seeing as how they weren't consecrated, no real harm's been done," he glanced directly at her, "on purpose."

His final instruction after the lesson was to pray harder for guidance. So when she left his study she headed for the chapel. In the gray hall she carried her humiliation of being a year behind the others and having to be tutored privately in silence.

Still the mysteries of rituals perplexed her. Eluding her was the nature of holiness, the realm of body and soul, the subtle distinction of when innocence became sin. The more she thought about these things the more confused and full of doubt she became. She chose the Station of the Cross where Jesus rested on one knee under his burden. Never had she been able to pray to the life-size blue and white Virgin and Child; they looked at each other with no need of anyone, she thought. Instead she had always come to this scene where the man looked down in weariness, his head bent from the cross, the crown of thorns staining his shoulders with blood.

"I'm sorry," she spoke to this statue, "I don't understand all the things they tell me about you," then sighing, she began her recitation of prayers that Father William had suggested.

When the dinner bell announced that they be seated, Ginger poked her in the ribs. "Jiggers," she whispered, "Something's up. Two extra monitors. Someone's in for it."

"It can't be me," Kate replied, "I said all the prayers exactly as I was instructed to," and a sweet calm swept over her.

At the far end of the room a bell sounded. Sister Mary stood her full height on the platform. "It has come to my attention that there is among us a most disgusting person." The room buzzed with disapproval which she stopped by ringing the bell. "Yes, unfortunately it is true. I am fully aware of this person, who, though she is provided with good food, negligently, and sinfully too I may add, sees fit to dispose of it. When I think of all the Lord's starving creatures in the world to whom one piece of bread would appear as a banquet, then do I realize the magnitude of this waste." Again the room hummed until stilled by the bell. "But, I am willing to be gracious if this person will come before me right now, stand in front of me and ask for my forgiveness. That is all the guilty one must do."

Kate recognized herself immediately as being the guilty one yet she could not move. What had seemed simple became a monstrous act. She expected to see Sister Mary's figure bearing down in her direction, that all eyes would be centered on herself but everyone sat squirming at the table while the room was filled with excitement.

The bell rang. "All right," Sister Mary's voice was now edged with anger, "I'm not surprised to find honesty lacking in this type of individual. I repeat," and Kate saw the nun stare in her direction, "I know who she is; however, if she is too shy to stand before us, she may see me later. She has until seven tonight and if she has not shown herself by then the punishment will have to come from those higher than we. That is all."

"Translation," said Ginger, "She doesn't know who did it, and can't do a blame thing except make this place feel more like Sing-Sing." Nodding towards the monitor walking down the aisle behind them, she added, "Such divine food, Kate. That creep must be out of her mind to pitch it away."

Another bell sounded to signal the bringing of food in from the kitchen. Grace was said. From now on she would eat everything placed in front of her including this bowl of potato soup.

"Oh, oh, " Ginger moaned, "I'd sure hate to be in your shoes just the same. Now it's up to that angel."

Kate remembered how Sister Mary had told them once that there was an angel with fiery wings, with a face terrible to behold who struck down those who defied, those who sinned. He came in a whirlwind around the middle of the night. She spooned the lukewarm soup swimming in globs of grease into her mouth, swallowing lumps of potatoes which did not dissolve.

That night, just before the dormitory lights were switched off for the night, she borrowed Ginger's scapular. "Pin it over your heart," her friend advised. Inside the holy object, the drop of Christ's blood would protect her. Wearing this the angel must show kindness. Kate was uneasy in the darkness so she began telling jokes, singing snatches of songs until one of the nuns came in warning that any further noise would result in losing their auditorium rights for a week. Grumbling, the children settled down. By the time she had said her prayers the room was quiet. In spite of the two blankets she was cold. Her cubicle was on the end and now she could make out the window frame. The wind moaned outside in the courtyard. Her wrists began to throb. It was as if it had all started when she had defied Sister Mary and had gone down that hill so quickly she could not stop. Because she could not quiet her doubt, her rebellion, she must face this terrible angel. Why were they all so harsh? Why was there no gentleness of the man, Jesus, in these women who dressed in black? They were always telling her to pray and thinking of that she climbed out of bed to kneel by the window. A draft of air chilled her and the blackness in the courtyard was frightening. She raised her eyes to the heavens seeking a bright star for her prayers. Low flying clouds skidded across the sky; dapple gray horses hid all stars.

A great black figure loomed out of the west. She watched to see how the angel would come to her, but the cloud trailed off like a wisp of smoke. Down the hall she heard a door slam so she ran to peek out into the corridor. A red eye stared back from the shadows at the far end of the hall, a dragon, she felt. Back to the window she ran seeking some sign, some star. Blackness and the noises of night-wind made her tremble. She asked herself why did she feel so terrible and the answer came back that she had to face the angel who was coming for her because she was a sinner, defiant out of the wildness in her blood. If she would not submit to the discipline of Sister Mary then she would have to face the one who was coming. A pane of glass shook as though a storm had come upon the land. Surely the time of his appearance was near. The angel would expect her to be kneeling, bowing her head in fright, but thinking this, she remembered the man chained by his wrists to the rock. She must find a way to talk to the angel to tell him she was not a sinner. What if he did not come? There were angels because there was God, she stilled the doubt. Once again she knelt by the window but with her head held high she waited. She would never know a night so long, so filled with sky figures, looming immensities which caused her dread inside to shriek like the wind. She waited in that aching black cold and when at last it was morning she knew that there was no angel coming to punish her. The darkness where she had sought stars was now inside. Out of that hollowness the voice of doubt had not been silenced.

She unpinned the scapular, carefully pulling the thread which held the seam. A small paper fluttered to her feet. Holding it to the light she saw on the silver tissue a dark spot. There was a drop of blood on this one. She slipped the paper back, knotted the thread. There was something she had to find out and later that morning when no one was looking, she slipped the box of scapulars down the front of her uniform and walked out of the store. Going to the shower room, deserted at this hour, she put the box on the floor then sat down. She pulled open another cotton heart and out fell a piece of silver tissue with the rust spot; another, and another, she tore open the hearts which lay like fallen petals by her side. Who could have gathered drops of blood from the foot of the cross? Was Christ not a natural man? Father William had said that He was a man mortal as himself. No man could have held so many drops of blood, her doubt spoke. With all the prayers, all the bells for rituals, they had lied to her. Now she could feel her anger thrashing into life. She tore open every single heart, left them for all to see on the shower floor, that they were nothing but snowflakes, star ashes. She went quickly from there into the chapel, to the Station of the Cross where Christ rested on one knee. This time she did not stop here but moved to the scene where He hung lifeless, death closing the gentle eyes of the man who understood.

"I waited all night to tell your angel that I was sorry for all my mistakes. And that I love you," and she felt the inner cold from last night chilling her. The eyes of the statue were closed. Falling in silence around her were silver snowflakes, star ashes which scattered where the nuns would walk; anointing their hands in holy water as lifeless as this blood, they would finger their beads through eternity. As she passed, the Virgin smiled sweetly at the fat babe in her arms; light flickered over her plaster face from the candles of the religious. The faithful would echo forever the responses in this nave.

Kate moved out of the chapel with clenched fists, out from under the constant red vigil hung over the altar. Inside, the hollowness tightened her breath with pain. She walked down the corridor towards what had been on that terrible night the eye of a dragon. She saw a red bulb over the word, EXIT. A cold wind blew through the infinite darkness within her where no star would ever shine.

45

Age of Reason

A Gift of Kindling IV

Karen knew that Ralph Martin had given her the marionette theatre, and Billy the English fort in order to make him their friend when he came calling on their mother. She liked him for spending time with them. One night, she had been telling him about the teachers at Miss Helane's School, when her mother interrupted. "Ralph," she had chided, "You'll spoil them." "Knowing your children, is knowing you," he had smiled and it brought back to Karen memories of her father. Since his death, seven years ago, the house was so strange. During holidays, when they returned from the private schools, their mother was gone. Mrs. Nash, the housekeeper, insisted they use the playroom, banished them from the "adult rooms", as she called them. The marriage had come as a surprise to the children, placing their mother in their midst suddenly when for years she had never come close to them. She had never appeared on visiting days, or when there were special programs put on by the students. They had told their friends how beautiful their mother was, how much she loved them, to conquer the silence she left them in. After the honeymoon, Ralph Martin had suggested that instead of sending them off to camp, the children be allowed to remain in the house for the summer. This is what gave Karen the idea of putting on a play for the occasion. Mrs. Nash had errands to do in town and the house was empty. Their parents were never home till five. She had persuaded Billy to help her carry the marionette theatre and props downstairs to their parents' room where a large mirror hung over the dresser.

"It's still not in the center," Karen told her brother, "Wait," she put her shoulder against the mahogany bed but the rug held it fast. "Help me, Billy," she said, "I can't do it alone."

"Are you sure Mama won't mind?" he asked.

"Of course not. What harm are we doing? Besides, you thought it was a swell idea. This way we can watch the play as the audience too. Come on, push."

Her brother did not move but shifted his weight from one foot to the other. At nine he was skinny, frail and prone to severe colds which she always mothered.

"Dad won't mind," she said, "After all he's the one who gave it to us." It pleased her that she had called him that.

"Ralph gave it to you," Billy scowled.

She knew why he was upset. Her brother had cut the fort that they might use sections of it for stage props. Their stepfather had teased Billy for playing with dolls, but then one day she had jumped from the dining table and he had called her a tom-boy, saying that if they could change their characters around it would be perfect. He had made their mother laugh though and she had defended them. "They have wonderful imaginations, that's all, Ralph."

"He's not so bad," Karen said to him, "If only you'd give him a chance. He is our father now because he married Mama."

"He's not like Papa and I shall always call him Ralph," said Billy.

"What do you know about Papa?" she shouted, "You were only two when he died." She was angry that he brought back the past. "It isn't as if he were a dragon or something." She bit her lip to hold in her tears.

"Don't be angry with me, Karry," Billy said, "I'm sorry."

He came over and the two of them were able to move the bed into the corner, out of the reflection of the mirror.

There, thought Karen, looking over the top of the theatre at the scarlet box, the stage, there is the world I know and love. Billy plugged in the wires lighting the velveteen curtain, blue embossed with gold masks of comedy and tragedy. With the shades drawn, their parent's room took on a forest quality, the deep green gloom giving it a strange new dimension. She reached into the prop box to choose the puppets she would work.

"Billy," she said, "The title of my play is 'The Kingdom Of Celebration'."

They took turns presenting the plays which they made up as they went along. "I got my people. Pick yours and we'll begin."

"Yes," her brother said and he reached for the old man. She saw the dull silver gleam of the knight, Sir Guilbert, he always chose him as champion. He always picks the same player, the same role, she thought. Again she felt annoyance with her brother. She wondered if there were not some way she could surprise him.

"What's it called again?" he asked, straightening the strings to the puppet.

" 'The Kingdom Of Celebration'. Come on, they'll be back before we ever get going. The first scene is in the forest — from there we'll switch directly to the palace. Enter the old couple."

He stopped, looked over at the bed in the shadows. "Maybe it's not such a good idea, I mean, maybe we shouldn't play in here."

"Oh, you sissy," she said, "Would I get us in trouble? I tell you it's safe." It seemed that she always had to remind him of how she cared for him. "Think of how pleased they'll be when we present our play in their honor. Look," she reached for the drawbridge of the fort, "This is perfect for scene five." The dust she stirred in the box of scenery made him sneeze.

"Okay," he finally agreed.

She began setting the stage, then peered over the top. "The audience is in their seats, the house-lights are being dimmed..." she dropped her hand to signal him to turn off the bedside lamp. "All set?" and he nodded.

Not until she had her marionette in front of the stage lights did she realize that she had the wrong one; the cloven hoof, a glint of his animal appearance as he made his bow. Somehow or other his cloak had been turned inside out, revealing black like the ringmaster, even his horns had been carefully covered by the top hat. It was too late to turn back, stop the show, the whole tradition of their theatre urged her on.

"Ladies and gentlemen," she made the devil touch the stage, knocking the top hat off at once.

"Oh," she heard Billy's surprise, "That's not the ringmaster."

She hissed for him to be quiet for once the show began they had made it a rule to speak only through their puppets. "Ah," she went on, letting the devil boot the hat off into the darkness, "I see that my poor attempt at a masquerade has failed. You know me for what I am. But do not hiss me, for I too am but a player worked by those above." She tilted his head back, had him finger the strings. "On with the play called, 'The Kingdom Of Celebration'. The time is long ago. The king of a foreign country has been dead for seven years and the people are sad. Today, though, the queen is getting married and her loyal subjects come from all around bearing gifts. As the curtain opens, we find a forest near the castle. Bertrand and Jeanette enter. Fiat lux." She withdrew the devil. Still the curtain did not rise. "Fiat lux," she repeated, "Let there be light," she said indignantly to Billy who began pulling back the curtain.

Karen looked over the top to the mirror where she saw the backdrop of blue-greens, the two tree trunks dividing the stage to suggest a forest. The effect was right, a depth, a silence, the audience spellbound in their seats, she hoped. Billy worked Bertrand in from the left, an old man, white beard, struggling under his bundle of kindling. When he reached the first tree, she moved the old woman onto the stage after him.

"Wife, in the old days the castle did not seem this far. My bones hurt from carrying this stack of wood. We should have given the queen goosefeathers for stuffing the royal mattress. Rest awhile," Billy gently worked the puppet's knees that he might sit.

"You cut it yourself. It's the best gift we can give," said Karen, her voice pitched low, trying for a hollowness of age. "And your aches for carrying it, is part of the gift, husband." She felt pleased with this line. On the marionette stage she never had trouble finding the correct words to say. Her puppet she made to rest next to Bertrand. Usually they chose the older people to speak through, made them gentle, full of concern for each other. Her favorite, though, was the ringmaster because his eyes reminded her of her father when he used to smile. Billy always enjoyed most being Sir Guilbert. Now her brother began moving the old man's head from side to side.

"Listen," he whispered, "The forest is so still, only the leaves tremble, no bird sings. Ever since the king died it has been sad in this forest. Today I do not feel safe here. I think evil must be afoot."

Karen was getting an idea. "Too bad," she said, "That Sir Guilbert is dead too, else he would have taken us safely to the castle."

"Dead?" echoed Billy. Plainly she had shocked him. He looked down at the silver clad knight waiting his cue.

"It came to me in a dream, husband," she went on, "Though he was the most valiant of the king's knights and he fought bravely, the fire-spitting dragon snapped him in two." She saw her brother licking his lower lip, trying to figure what to say, what to do. Then she selected the marionette used as the princess. "Ha!" she spoke, letting her drop with a clatter in front of the couple, "I am the evil fairy. Whereas you see only my loveliness, yet am I the evil one. The woods are not safe from such as me. Indeed the castle itself, no matter that a new king comes to rule."

"We are simple people, a woodcutter and his wife, bearing a gift for the wedding," Billy said.

The little doll's face twinkled with her smile, Karen moved her in dancing steps about the stage. "I will never touch either one of you. If you believe the kingdom is good, far be it from me to set you straight. Simple people think simple things." She was made to fly up from the stage as quickly as she had come.

"This is where Sir Guilbert would help us if he knew," said Billy looking sadly at the knight.

Karen bent close to his ear. "Remember the night we got scared watching TV? The ghost? Why don't you bring him on as one?"

He gave her a big smile, picked up his puppet. "Look, Jeanette, isn't that Sir Guilbert's ghost coming through the forest?" The long sword at the knight's side caught on his spur which sent him tripping onto the stage. "Greetings, old people. I have come to escort you to the castle. Although I am no longer of this world, I do not forget my duty to my king's subjects."

She could see how happy her brother was with this arrangement. She picked up the old woman, advanced to the footlights. "Pst. Ladies and gentlemen, know that when a ghost walks, it is the hand of the devil. All say that this is a time of celebration, but be not too sure. As Bertrand says, 'evil is afoot'."

"Karen," Billy said, "What are you doing? That's not fair talking to the audience. Sir Guilbert has the right to rescue us. You're not playing fair."

"Fair?" she said, "What's that? This is the devil's play," Here she broke into a cackling laugh. "Who knows what he's about?" There was no doubt in her mind that she had surprised her brother by first mistaking the devil for the ringmaster, then by telling him that Sir Guilbert was dead.

'I don't want to play any more with you," he said, forgetting their rule about speaking to each other during a performance.

The pretty face of the fairy smiled at her, the devil mocked. "And I don't care to play with you. A boy playing with dolls. Sissy!" she spat the word in his face. "Afraid of the forest," she saw his face come loose, the jaw drop, the eyes drop for the tears to come. "Cry baby to boot. Afraid of ghosts, afraid to play in Mama's room. Bah," she threw down her puppet. "Play by yourself."

"All right," Billy straightened himself as tall as he could, "I don't need you anymore, ever."

She ran out of the bedroom, down the hall, slamming the front door behind her. She kicked the gravel with her toe, hearing it fall, as when rain strikes quickly. They had broken their own rules of the game. Well, why not? Life had no rules that she could understand. She was surprised to discover that she was crying also. Everything seemed to have gone wrong. She should have felt happy that now they had a father, that was what she had been trying to say in her play but Billy was stubborn, would not let go of what he remembered. Their mother was as beautiful as the princess, she deserved a new king, didn't she? And now she would be close to them, closer than ever before in her life. Yet why did she still seem so far away? And she loved Billy, she was the one who had cared for him always but today she felt so mean. Play fair, he had shouted at her as if she had made the rules. Why did he expect them to be the same? Always he wanted to be Sir Guilbert, and again she felt her anger. It was to have been a happy play, "The Kingdom Of Celebration", and he had ruined it. Up at the window she saw her brother peeking at her. She stuck her tongue out, saw the shade fall shut. Afraid of evil, afraid of ghosts, what would happen if he really had to meet one without her? She looked up at the pale sky. What if one were to drop from it as the evil fairy had dropped onto the stage? The window opened.

"Karry?" Billy called, "Don't be mad. Let's start again."

She dashed behind a spruce tree knowing he was watching. "What are you doing?" he asked.

"Billy, it's here," she called, "Run!"

"What?" he was searching the yard for what she had seen.

She ran over to the next tree where he could not see her from the window, and from here she let herself in the back door of the house. She could hear him calling her. Taking her skirt up to her mouth, she screamed into it, "Ghosts." Now he was running from the bedroom into the hall.

"Karry? Where are you?"

She made not a sound, not yet, as she waited. He must still be standing there listening for she could not hear him moving. Served him right for telling her that he did not need her. She brought her foot forward with a crash, then the other.

"Karry?" he called again.

Taking two more steps, she moved towards the door leading to the hall. Opening her mouth, she screamed as hard as she could. His steps were heard going upstairs, slipping in his haste. Go ahead, lock yourself in, she thought, possessed by the spirit of the game she was playing. In her mind was a horror film she had seen on TV where a stiff-legged ghost, slashed across the face, moved like a doll. She imitated his robot style down the hall, up the stps. The empty house echoed from her brother's cries in his bedroom, her pounding feet. Even when she heard the car drive onto the gravel, she could not stop; somehow his screams were inside her, driving her on. The front door opened below, steps were coming behind her. Then it was that her fear blasted wide open, she forgot the game in that house which was strange to her, which no longer felt safe like home. Her panic drove her to Billy's door. "Let me in, hurry. They're behind me." She tore her fingernails across the wood but he held his body against her assault, screaming out her cries with his own.

Ralph Martin had raced up the steps to grab her to him and she struck him on the face. The coldness of his look brought her to her senses. She tried to call him Dad, only the name would not come out. He pushed open the door. Immediately Billy stopped screaming. "I hate you," he sobbed, his wet cheeks, eyes mute with terror filled Karen with shame.

"Ralph?" their mother called from the stairs.

"In here," the man said.

She is so beautiful, thought Karen, even in anger she is beautiful but she did not know how to reach out, to touch her mother.

"Ralph?" she had reached her husband and placed the black velvet glove on his arm. "What happened?"

"Don't ask me," he said. "They were both yelling their heads off and when I put my arm around your daughter," he paused, fingered his cheek where she had scratched him.

"Darling," their mother said, going over to him, kissing his cheek. "Why there's blood." She turned to face them. Karen could not meet her fury; she lowered her eyes. Billy was sobbing. "I have given you children everything," she began slowly, "Everything. I have devoted my life to you. When your father died I sacrificed that you might go t the best schools, be deprived of nothing. And this is the thanks I get. Ralph, whom I love dearly, married me. It was his idea to let you stay in the house, to let you get to know him as your new father. Instead this is how you repay us." She put her arm around the man's waist while they watched, saying nothing. From her pocket she drew a handkerchief into which she began sobbing. Karen smelled the Shalimar. The man drew her close to him.

"Come," he kissed her ear, "I'm sure they'll explain later. They love you dearest," he said. One of them should have picked it up as if it were a cue, we love you, we have always loved you, shouting it over the boundless distance she moved from them, but there was only silence, deep as the forest, deep as their game, a thing of disaster. The man led her downstairs, away from them.

Karen knew she had betrayed Billy; she had repeated what their mother had always done with them when she allowed them to come close, close enough to feel their need, their love seeking some way to express itself toward her, only then she laughed, teased them, pushing them back upon themselves, back upon the past. Essentially their mother would always be the stranger in the house. All the things of the past that Karen remembered, even that dim memory of her father, she had betrayed by this performance, by this evil in her heart. Inside, in deep green depths, she felt the coldness of unborn tears for all her love that her mother denied.

"Karry," Billy gasped, "the theatre..."

It was too late to go into their parents' room. They stood at the top of the stairs, listening. They could hear voices, the sound of something being broken. Soon they heard him shoving the theatre into the hall; only then did they go down to look. The marionette theatre was so small, so fragile, the blue curtain was ripped. Sir Guilbert lay twisted, broken in two as if he were smashed by a dragon. The princess she had used for the evil fairy lay in the arms of the devil, clasped in an embrace, meshed by their strings, her smile ever beautiful as his face pressed to her heart.

Muskrat V

The pond, though it was small, sustained a multitude of life.
Living in the old house on the east side, Margaret Pearson took
pleasure noting the wild birds, some of whom stayed awhile to
fish from slender weeds; the creatures who drank, sheltered by
the grass so that their muzzle ripples might have appeared as a
trout, or bass, or one of the pike, the legendary pike the old-
timers talked of in the village. The pike could be seen sometimes
in summer from the River Road lying like submarines in the
depths of brown water. She had spent most of her life in cities
until coming to Vermont three years earlier when her husband
was so ill and this hollow by the pond seemed a lost wilderness.
His death had given her a sense of desolation which she tried to
overcome by studying all the natural life surrounding her.
Because she had no children, she welcomed each one who
wandered in the woods in search of puffballs, or spring flowers,
and who had found her door.

As she hung the clothes in the yard, she looked past the lawn
bordered by goldenrod at how silvery the willow grew towards
the end of summer until it reached this filigreed languor, yet
there were times when the pale buds blossomed with as many
birds as buds above the water like a pagoda; or, later, how in
autumn winds, the tree metamorphosed into a ship's mast
creaking with the tensions of ropes and tackles. She had seen the

pond whipped into frenzy like a minute storm-tossed sea. To live quietly in this place observing its changes gave her a sense of something being eternal, beyond the limits of sickness and death.

This morning, the children on their way to school on the River Road caught her eyes as their bicycles flashed in the sun; a red one ridden by a boy with fair hair came close to the pond.

"A muskrat," he yelled. "Heh, look. A muskrat!"

Two boys joined him looking down at the ripples where the muskrat was swimming; then they all rode off. There were two muskrats in the pond. She had watched them making innumerable trips to store the green grasses under the stump of a dead tree.

The October afternoons were warm and she worked to get the storm windows up, gather wood for the shed for evening fires. An oil furnace was installed when she had moved in but she enjoyed reading books in front of the grate now that she had time; nothing new, nothing of war, or cruelty, or brute strength; she chose instead to find those who remained human in spite of adversity, that rare discovery as if she had come across some dear, lost friend. A woman has need of simple, everyday things that continue, she believed, so she shut out the chaos, the implied destruction of the world today by working in the garden when the weather permitted, feeding the birds that inhabited the pond and its margins and by reading at the fire in the evenings.

That fall, the fair-haired boy with the red bike played frequently across the pond. Usually she saw him in the afternoons and one day she swung her binoculars from the woodpecker as the boy paused by a stake. He pulled on a chain attached to a trap. From the dead tree, out to the point, she realized that he had laid a series of them. She went close to the water and called, "This is private property, no hunting, or trapping."

He scrambled up the bank to his bike. "You don't own the pond."

Not long after this, as she was shopping in the local store, a man dressed in plaid shirt, khaki pants, muttered as she passed, "Too damn bad a kid can't hunt or trap no more without no woman hollerin'." He was answered by someone down the aisle that they'd like to see them stop his kid, or himself, for that matter.

The snow came early that December with temperatures dropping below zero, freezing over the pond except for the black channel water. More than ever she enjoyed the old house set in the hollow, protected by the trees whose naked tops snapped together in the frigid blasts on the ridge. A pair of cardinals remained like brilliant tropical birds to sit at the feeder, joining the grosbeaks, the purple finches and blue jays in festivals of color. The ice, thawed, refroze against the banks with cracks and rumblings as it shifted. The stakes disappeared but not the boy. After an absence of two weeks he was back, chopping through the ice to see if he had caught anything.

The birds emptied the feeders quickly in winter and as she was filling one, she heard the chopping stop. "Heh, lady," the boy's voice reached her. Coming down to the willow she faced him. He dangled something above his head. Without glasses she could not distinguish what it was. "Catch," he laughed, and by the still dark body he threw over the ice, she knew it was the muskrat.

That night she could not sleep for thinking of how it had lived in the pond, and the senseless killing by the boy angered her. After breakfast she tried to telephone the game warden. He did not answer. By the second day she made an effort to call every other hour until finally in the evening she was able to speak with him only to learn that traps could be set providing they were inspected daily.

"They aren't inspected," she said. "The boy put them in the fall. It was two weeks before he came near them."

Something in his voice implied that she had disturbed him over the relative unimportance of a few muskrats and she could hear his insolence when he promised to investigate shortly.

She took to leaving bread, bits of raw vegetables by the willow to keep the other one alive, away from traps. The boy did not come any more. She kept a vigil all through the long winter but neither boy nor warden came.

After the first thaw sent the water crashing over the falls near the entrance of her road, so much water that the windows rattled in their casements like rifle fire against cannonade, she knew the silence of snows was over.

One week in March she noticed a tomato colored station wagon stop on the River Road and a man went out to the point. She put on her jacket, went out to speak to him. "Hello," she called, "Are you the warden?"

The man was stocky. He did not look up from the stakes he was pounding. "Nope." He placed eight stakes without looking in her direction.

She saw a strand of blond hair under the cap, and she recognized the voice of the man from the store who swore about trapping. "The warden is checking this pond for illegal trapping," she said hoping to scare him off.

"I just come today," he lied, for he had staked the traps there since October.

She went back inside, took all the curtains down to wash so the anger could dissipate in activity, determined to phone the warden if he did not inspect them within twenty-four hours.

The following morning she was awakened by barking from the pond. A frantic howl sent her quickly dressed around the house to the willow. Two dogs stood in the water by the point of land. They did not move but were rooted and the painful howl reminded her of the metal teeth below the water. She drove her car out of the hollow, past the falls, crossing the bridge to the other side. She scrambled down the bank, her face, arms and legs scratched by brambles. Cold water soaked through her mocassins. It was not the dog who was trapped. Rearing, she saw the small muskrat draw back his lips to hiss. The two mongrels backed out of reach of the green-stained teeth. Picking up a stick, she yelled, "Go home." One growled but she brought the stick down with a whack on the water splashing them so they circled off to the bank. The muskrat sank into the dark water to swim and she saw the bone jutting above where the teeth had clamped on the right hind paw. She managed to get the stick in while the creature thrashed, heaved itself loose. The mongrels raced alongside the pond but she shouted and raised the stick at them. The ripples ended at the willow fringe where the muskrat had gone.

Furiously she went to each stake snapping the traps and pulling each one out, she hurled them into the underbrush. After driving home, she spent three hours telephoning the warden who finally answered.

"Lady," he snapped, "I'm on vacation this week."

"Suppose that had been the dog in the trap?" she said and when he did not answer, she realized it would have made no difference to him, dog or muskrat. "What if it had been a child playing who stuck his foot in it?"

"It wasn't," he said. "In emergencies you can always call Charley Russell," and giving her the number, he hung up.

Charley Russell lived sixty miles north but he drove down the next morning. He was a young man in his twenties, standing straight in his uniform similar to a trooper's, he listened quietly as she told him of the pond, what lived on it, and how the boy had thrown the dead muskrat at her. "He didn't even want it," she said. "I understand a man trapping for food, or for the living he can make out of the fur. I'm afraid I got so angry at this cruelty that I pulled all the traps out and threw them on the bank."

"Did you notice if there was a metal license with his name on the traps?" he asked.

When she confessed that she had not, he suggested they ride over to find them. "You know, if they are licensed, I'm afraid you're the one who has broken the law by interfering with game traps." His honest face frowned, looked straight ahead of him.

She led him through the brambles to where she had pitched the eight traps.

"Frank Bromley," he read, "West Road. They're legal."

The injustice of her having broken the law was too much for her. Legal. How was it legal to put a cruel-teethed trap in water and leave it unchecked for weeks at a time because no one bothered? No one cared for something as small, as unimportant as a muskrat. The rocket race to the moon and the nuclear umbrella of destruction made small the natural laws of conservation. "What if it had been a dog?" she had asked, "Or a child?"

"You were right to call me," the warden said, "But I can't do anything about this. First, I would have to see the traps placed, keep them under observation, catch him illegally in the act if he did not check them within twenty-four hours. Vermont is small as states go but I have to cover a lot of territory. This isn't even my area."

She knew he did not owe her an explanation, that officially he had to inspect the complaint in another district but he did not treat it as a troublesome duty, nevertheless, she saw how the teeth of the trap could function freely, while the law had no enforcement; that a man, or child could set himself above it to fish, hunt, or trap whenever he would regardless of it. By ruthlessness he could even exterminate a breed, or species at his whim. Holding the trap in her hand, she said nothing.

"We call them 'woodchucks'," he went on, "the ones who know the law but who don't care. There are streams, once filled with trout, with nothing but suckers. They use powerful flashlights at night to blind the deer, doe or buck, makes no difference. I've seen the carcasses on the mountain when they get through. I've found sheep and dogs starved to death because no one came to inspect the traps. 'Woodchucks'."

She tried to respect and take comfort from his words, his uniform, all he stood for, but he was only one man in an area where the land was bountiful with wild life. There were the others, the "woodchucks", he had called them, who killed in what manner they could.

The warden drove her back to the hollow and she thanked

him. After he left, she made a decision. She drove back to where he had put the traps. Carefully she collected them. On the ridge behind her house she buried them deep in the earth, covering them with moss to rot among the leaves that fell year after year. As long as she lived here she knew that the pond would be her responsibility; that if it were not possible to apprehend the man who took the law unto himself, who would ever guess that it was simply a woman who wanted the ripple of a muskrat to continue to spread over the pond, unending as the waves of the sea, or the flight of birds across the sky?

63

Muskrat

"Ich Liebe Dich" VI

At one time of my life I lived in Spain but I have found that when I say this to some people I get a curious reaction, almost childish, some sly look, some knowing look as if they based my life on what they had read in Hemingway's "The Sun Also Rises", or God knows what story. For them I think the word Spain stands for some earthly paradise of romantic love, of easy life, a place uncharted, unspoiled. When I get this look, I never hasten to tell them any more. It is just that when I look back upon this time when I was twelve, the world seemed new; a life rich in truth which had its start at the Villa Santa Maria, a pensión near Barcelona in the year 1936. To this day I am haunted from that past because what was true then can just as well be true today, tomorrow, therefore in my mind it has become an absolute, an essence of life, how man behaves, what he feels for himself and the others in the world around him. Each sunset sees this world shrinking closer to him. I would answer those sophisticated ones of the sly leer by reminding them of that quality of courage which Hemingway gave his hero. True, the man lived with the brass taste of fear in his mouth, the trembling under pressure, the doubt, the solitude. Once in an English class after I had returned to this country, the high school teacher had to approve our compositions, and when I said I would like to do mine on Spain, he looked blank. "Why Hemingway has done Spain," he told

65

me, "why not write of your impressions of the trip home after those strange years over there." There was such finality, such desolation in the manner he used that word, done. I did not say to him that it was my home I had left, that now I was a stranger in the land of my birth for he would not have understood.

Spain was home to me at that time, granting me citizenship with each bombing, each killing in the streets, and the dark quaking fear I inherit, which is underneath, the roots of my being. Twelve is a child to most people, for the outward appearance is small, but I remember the trembling inside me was great, already more of womanhood than of that lesser, playful world. So it was at the threshold of my life that the world blew itself up in civil war; from then on the nightmare shared equal rights with sweet sleep, part of me, though, never slept, but kept alert in dark places. At twelve it was fairy tale magic to battle hidden monsters in the safety of your own bed for who ever died from a nightmare?

At this age of reason, I lived in the Villa Santa Maria, resembling its namesake, the gallant ship of Columbus, with its oak beams inside, balconies overlooking the bay of the city below. When the wind blew off the mountain of Tibidabo, the whole structure creaked as if setting sail under the masts; the resin from the pines added to this illusion. Surrounding the pensión was a garden with flowers, date palms, sealed from the street by a wall lined with pieces of broken bottles which the Spaniards use to discourage those who would enter other than through the gates. I would play in this lush garden, catching bugs, lizards to put in boxes.

Once or twice a week my mother took me into Barcelona by trolley or metro to shop, for Sarría, where we lived, was but a suburb. It was a beautiful city with its churches, wide plazas, the bull ring. On the Ramblas, a tree-lined thoroughfare, the people would promenade, shop, sit at the cafés with their papers, their books, and talk. I can remember seeing soldiers in loose red trousers, wound in sashes, black men from some African legion; the English were there in pressed white suits, an immaculate

PAT

BECK

colony, and lately, more it seemed with each passing week, the tall blond Germans marched the length of the Ramblas, cameras about their necks, calling themselves, "tourists". I would watch them buying German newspapers at the kiosk where I got "Crackers", an English comic sheet. There were some who had women with them, massive they seemed to me; I imagined that if I were accidentally to bump into one, their flesh would be as hard as a man's. Their eyes looked as if this were true. So tightly was their long hair drawn to the back of their heads in a bun, it seemed they could not smile.

Yet I went riding on my bike with a boy called Hans who had none of this stiffness about him. His eyes were merry, black laughing eyes above such red cheeks and his teeth were white. I loved him for this beauty, following him wherever he rode till one day he waited for me, shook my hand, and from then on we were together. Now that I think of it I wonder how such a bond grew between us for Hans did not speak English or Spanish, and I knew no German. We smiled, liked what we saw in each other; it was enough.

Besides Hans there was Rudy, another German boy, Toby from Wales, Jane from Capetown and Ortegá. On the right hand side of the front wheel of our bicycles each of us fastened a small flag from the country of our birth. Sometimes we went high up the mountain, leaving our bikes below, while we sought out a shepherd for songs. We made kites to fly high against Tibidabo, resting under pines to drink gaseosa, a cheap lemon soda, eat our chunks of break, soaked in olive oil, with sausage. The time was too short for us; we were always having to part. Then one day Hans gave me a lesson in German, so simple, so pure that its innocence became a white light I carried inside and being still part of that world of childhood I turned to tell my mother that she would feel proud of me, that I had been accepted, no longer unlovable as she made me feel.

At breakfast the next morning over my cup of chocolate I tried to tell her, but she was in a hurry, she was busy, later, later. Again at noon it went the same way so that it was not until bedtime when I refused to go unless she listened to this wonderful thing which had happened. "All right," she sighed, her face wearing the look of martyrs seen on stained glass panels, which is the way I see her now that she is long since dead. "All right. What is it?"

"Hans," I said, "taught me to say, 'Ich liebe dich' ".

I know how I must have looked to her with that open trust, the unguarded barrier which must have shown her that I was no longer simply a child.

I have never forgotten the feel of her hand across my mouth, nor the word she spit at me, the pain terrible, going deep. No longer was my world innocent for I learned from her look that the heart must be hidden. My bike was taken away from me. Of course I was not allowed to see Hans. He did not go to my school. He was a boy who rode, who climbed, spending his life outside. If he ever came to the Villa Santa Maria, he must have been turned away. I did not see him again. I'm sure he tried to see me, but he was a free kind of soul who would ride off, say to some other girl what he had said to me. His beauty would open life for him.

From the fields, those games of childhood, now I had but dreams of loneliness under the broken glass wall where my mother insisted I stay. I took to wandering through the long halls of the pensión, curious about the people living behind so many doors. Pacó, a country boy who worked in the kitchen, when he carried jugs of water up to the rooms, would tell me their names. Don José, with his family of three children lived on the first floor that had bedrooms, living room with an out-of-tune piano, and the dining rooms. Don José owned the pensión, very fat, jolly, he ruled over his domain as king. Pacó was court fool, servant too poor of spirit to be fun, though, for his work took away his energy, leaving him surly and cruel. From this mood I learned effective words, abusing ones to start a fight, or by their insolence, protect me as one of the knowing, one who could pass untouched.

On the second floor I only got to know the students from the university, Miguel and Leon. Miguel was a dark Spaniard with a harmony of balance in his features like a statue. His father, and his father before him, far back to dust-laden centuries, had been doctors; not of the poor villages scrubbing off rock soil, but in prominent government posts, or in the court or military. He would smile at me, but it felt cold — his smile. Perhaps it was shyness. Always he carried a book under his arm, and when alone, he would immediately open it to shut off any communication.

Leon, his friend, studied law. Thick glasses seemed to weigh his head down so that he never met your gaze. His upper teeth protruded giving him an Oriental appearance, a studied withdrawal. Both were polite, firm with me. Once I told them there had been fighting in the south and I asked them whether they would give up their books to join the army.

Miguel spoke, not to me, but to Leon, "We fight with the keenest weapon of all, our minds." I could not help but admire this, yet in a way he disappointed me, for at twelve I saw how easily an idea becomes an ideal, a quest, a striving action which must culminate in a fight; from inside man must come the restoration of order to the chaos. A rebel who demanded action, that was me, a time when books are to be put aside, a time to act. Their studies seemed a trench of safety. I never knew whether they were greater heroes for sticking to what they believed, or whether I was right in my anger towards them for imposing their fight upon others.

Barcelona was changing in appearance. On the streets were more soldiers than I had ever seen. They were coming in from the country still wearing the rope-soled alpargatas instead of boots; some had ill-fitting tunics above their corduroy trousers, or khaki pants below a wool sweater; some with only an armband to constitute a uniform. These men roamed the streets of the city, their unrest hung as a summer storm darkens the horizon beyond a wheat field or arbor.

In school the excitement swept through us though we did not understand what was happening. We knew that the Rights were opposed to the Lefts. Overnight, posters would be pasted on buildings. On the Villa Santa Maria's wall one with a gold shield, four red stripes which symbolized the four fingers of blood from El Valiente Vifredo, the coat of arms of Cataluña, was found half destroyed. In our neighborhood these posters of the Rights were always mutilated. On the playground I learned the Rights were the royalists, Franco with his regiments of Moors on white Arabia steeds, their lances flashing in front of the steps of the cathedral where he, Franco reviewed them. This I saw in a newsreel but with such booing and hissing that when the audience began ripping apart the theatre, the screen went dark for a few minutes, then they showed a Mickey Mouse to quiet them. Most of the Rights were from the south, around Madrid, that part of Spain. Mostly the Catalans were Leftists, against what Franco stood for. To start a schoolroom fight one had simply to holler, "Arriba Franco" for the fists to fly, though with us it was a form of a game.

Heavy trucks rumbled through to the city raining clouds of dust as they passed through Sarria. There were rumors that the holy walls of Monserrat, pinnacled as they were, possessed cannon. We did not stop going into the city, for it was by now a habit of my mother's to have luncheon, a movie, a tour through the department stores followed by café on the Ramblas. It was on such a typical weekend evening, as we were nearing the Plaza Cataluña that the air suddenly became filled with buzzing, as though many mosquitoes hovered. As we got closer, the sounds were louder, a pattering now, hooves, many hooves clattering over cobblestones. The excitement of seeing horsemen made me push ahead, tugging at my mother to hurry that we not miss such a sight. Men were shouting up ahead around the plaza. My mother was trying to reach the entrance of the metro there. I remember seeing the leaves of the trees hanging in the streetlights so that half of them were silver where they were touched by the light, the other half in purple shadows. A horse neighed, frightening me for a second till I realized what it was.

I looked at my mother wondering at the tightness, the way her face seemed a stranger's. Then I caught the flash of silver against a pale blue sky, a sword raised by a man who stood high in the stirrups, who swung it up, where it stopped, came down below my vision into the darkness up ahead. This time the scream was prolonged, not of a horse but of a human being. I ran, stumbled at the side of my mother down the steps underground as the tide of cavalry swept inwards upon the plaza. When the train door slammed, the engine's whistle sickened me with its imitation of that scream.

The following weekend we did not go into the city for the paper warned of disturbances, that the cavalry patrolled areas so people could not congregate. A block away from the pensión, a machine gun rested behind sandbags pointed at a field where the weeds grew in rank disorder.

Conchita, the fat maid of our floor — filled with more news than any paper, is my friend. She is in love with our family and dreams we will take her with us to America when we return.

"Before I die I must meet Cluck Gablay," she says, pressing those peasant hands to her bosom. After many talks with her, trailing her into rooms, helping her make beds, empty water basins, I learn she is talking of Clark Gable.

"Tell me," she asks, "do the gankstars kill the men of feathers?" Knowing that recently at the Rivoli was a Jimmy Cagney film, that the Paramount featured a western, to me it is quite resonable she would see my country like this.

"I don't think so," I say, "I'm not sure. I live in New York."

"Ah, Nueva York," she smiles, off on some film, one I don't know but one I wish I had seen, for her look is beautiful, serene. To her, my country brings out this dream of loveliness in her face.

We go down the hall to deposit the dirty linen. "It is bad in the village of my sister," she goes slack in the jaw muscles. "A priest hangs butchered on hooks in the meat store, four pieces of him. Out front they fly his cassock." She tells it so clearly that in my mind I see the puddles of blood in the sawdust, but then I am used to blood in sawdust for on Sundays I am taken to the bull plaza with the rest of Barcelona. I did not seem to care what happened to the toreroes, for they flaunted insolence at the bull who had no fate other than to die. But once a horse was lifted high on those horns, ripping underneath the mattress I thought would protect him, ripping apart so he could no longer hold the fat picador whom they hoisted off. While a different mount was brought in, the bull charged the wounded horse again and again, the scent of blood urging him into fury. Though the horse no longer kicked, the tears streamed down my face. No one told me the horses would be hurt, they told me only the bull, once in awhile a torero would get flung, but it made him fight better next time. I drew jeers, calls of "cry baby" from the Spaniards seated about me. Listening to Conchita tell of the priest's blood, I tried to show her my new toughness. "Did he bleed much?"

"Not much. A priest is not much man," she shrugged.

At night, when the city should have been still, we could hear occasional rifle fire, machine gun bursts in response which carried off the bay, up the side of the mountain. One night I sat behind the garden walls, on a balcony looking down the street at nothing till three men came in sight. I could see they were some sort of soldiers when they passed beneath the streetlight. One wore a peaked cap pulled over his ear. They had their arms about each other singing. I saw one man take out his bayonet from the sheath at his hip, drive it down between the shoulder blades of the one in the middle. This man fell to his knees, head bent over the alpargatas of the one in the peaked cap who then kicked his jaw knocking him over. The one with the bayonet wiped it on the fallen one's tunic, replaced it at his side. He then took some things out of the man's pockets, who clutched his stomach, whose knees were drawn nearly to his chin in death agony. They divided what they wanted, threw some of the paper on him. "Boracho," the killer said as they hoisted him between them, dragging his body off the street into the field of darkness. They went off the street singing, the two of them. It was a time of madness, a time I could no longer understand.

When six Guardia Civil in their black patent leather helmets were posted outside the pension, it made my mother feel safer. "You see," she told my father, "our government demands the protection of its citizens. How soon will it be before we can leave here?"

My father for weeks had been negotiating passage but he would find different officials, different rules though they all had the same answer, "Mañana." My mother felt safe behind their bayoneted rifles, their inscrutable faces.

Conchita made me see their faces as belonging to beasts who were cruel, no longer aware of people's feelings, knowing only how to torture, to kill. She would spit, say it was a bad omen. One morning on my way to school I noticed they were gone; that evening she told me how they had taken Mrs. Albeniz as hostage since her husband did not show up. Mrs. Albeniz was a small birdlike woman who fed cookies to my Pekingese. When I asked what would happen to her, I was surprised at how this hard peasant woman cried. She made the sign of the cross, clutched me to her moaning, and I was glad I was not a woman led off by the Guardia Civil. I never knew what became of her, or her husband, who Conchita said had gone south to dynamite an ammunition train.

Now the pensión creaking in the wind no longer seemed a ship to sail out of this bay, the wall about it seemed to grow higher, grow broken glass like flowers making us prisoners in those dark halls where sometimes, in the shadows, I thought I saw a soldier waiting beyond the turn in the hall.

"Tomorrow," my father said, "tomorrow I shall be able to pick up our tickets. Ships are leaving all the time."

Meanwhile I went to school, joked with the soldiers behind the machine gun, but from the other side of the street for there was one who did not look me in the face; he always stared at my body. There was homework, math, declension of French verbs, while all around us in some part of the hills, or the city, bombs, cannon were going off, even in daylight.

Countess L., I forget her long Roumanian title, asked if our family would take her Armand to America for his bloodline should be carried on. Europe, she said sadly, would not have time to breed Pekingese. Armand was the meanest Peke I ever saw. We had two already, Fan-Toy, the mother, Mocha-Tan, the baby who was my dog. I did feel sorry for this lovely sable dog forced to sit the long hours she demanded of him on an embroidered velvet cushion. When she left, I brought him into my room, bent to kiss that silly flat head, but he snapped, cutting my cheek. For days Armand snapped when I tried to pet him.

My father came home triumphantly one day with the tickets in his hand for our passage the following week. When I knew we were really going, the fear seemed to grow stronger in me. At night I clutched Mocha to me against the terrors I imagined loose in that city gone mad. One night I awoke out of sleep to see below in the harbor a battleship, she was lit from stem to stern, poking the sky, the buildings with her searchlights. Only afterward did we learn Madrid had ordered this. High from the window I saw the burst of orange followed by grey smoke, then the thunder of the guns reaching me. It seemed to be happening so far away that it was as if I were watching a movie. My Girl Guide troop, supplied with bandages rode in ambulances down to that section which had been bombarded. Walls, chipped, without plaster stood among heaps of fallen buildings. I wondered what good was our gift of cotton for I saw only bodies piled on the curb, the blook looking black in the morning sun, too dirty for the fresh pieces of cloth. Besides they had no need for bandages.

At twelve I was to leave this world but as I say I was already more than a child, but glad I was not yet a woman. Germans, Italians, Americans poured in as we were leaving. They bled alongside the Spaniards on both sides, killing so many it was a miracle that there were any left. History has since taught us that it was only a dress rehearsal for the wars that were to follow.

By this time I was a woman, having learned from the Spaniard and my mother to conceal the heart, show only toughness. I hope I said goodbye bravely to family and friends who went off to fight. The old Peke, Armand proved sterile and he never did stop snapping at people; he was put out of his misery at thirteen, biting the vet's hand who went to give him the needle. This time I laughed in spite of the tears at silly old Armand.

From the haunted pensión of Santa Maria, the blood in the streets, the smell of death in that civil war accustomed me to these other wars involving many nations. My generation has become so tough, so sophisticated from what it has learned that now, if all else fails, there is the dreadful prospect to push a button which will cause a holocaust beyond my scope of suffering and despair. In this no-man-world of today, I still feel that somehow this can be avoided. It must be avoided. Perhaps, if I tell you, you will indicate that I am mad, maybe you are right; it has become my trench of safety. Or you will laugh, say it is just like a woman, but what I believe is this, that always the children are right when they breech language with what is in their hearts, that we should put faith in the newness that is always with them, the goodness which is theirs. Would this not be a place to start then, for surely to say "Ich liebe dich" to a stranger is not a sign of sin, but of salvation.

"Ich Liebe Dich"

"Kate O'Reilly, C'est Moi" VII

The leg was beginning to throb above the knee and twice within the hour had cramped at mid-calf. When Kate O'Reilly had entered the hospital it was to be simply a bed rest for the healing of an infected toe. She had forgotten the elaborate precautions a diabetic should expect. The I-V dripped antibiotics into her foot.

At her side, secured to the rail, was a brown canvas bag with her books. They were a comfort. Along with Merville's "Moby Dick", and Defoe's "Robinson Crusoe", she had a journal kept by one of her relatives. Also a friend had given her, "The Race To The South Pole", by William Bixby.

"I included a small atlas," he had told her, "so you can find your way in an alien land."

It was an alien land where Robert Scott and Ernest Shackleton among others had explored. She had almost finished reading the book on the Antarctic; much of the territory she was familiar with from the journal.

She reached for the journal of Paul Scope, otherwise known to her as Uncle Just. It was the black weather-beaten book he had carried around on all his journeys. Tiny insects had chewed their outlines on the paper. His handwriting, in faded black ink, was as fine as the lines of the insects so it was a puzzle sometimes to find out what he had written and where they had chewed their lives away. They too were writers, she smiled, always looking for a way to record, to preserve life to the fullest. The paper was rough under her fingers, its edges cream colored because they had been used first aboard the supply ship "Discovery". Her finger pinpointed a day, "14 February, 1907: I count myself one of the lucky members of this expedition as they brought back Jones and Henderson. Each man had lost several toes from gangrene. They had amputated themselves to keep the infection from spreading. God, it's cold enough on board. Don't see how they endure out there on those ice-floes."

She closed the journal, not wanting to read any more about the ice. Her eyes could not stay open and she felt herself slipping back in time. Her leg ached. It was all this jumping from rock to rock on the jetty to reach the end from where the whales could be seen best. The Gulf Stream approached here on its course past the Jersey shore. She had wonderful swims in October when the air nipped because of this stream of warm water. The summer people never dared the water after Labor Day, only the sun-worshippers and fishermen came to the beach. But she had grown up here during World War II when the family had moved to the summer house because it was smaller and cheaper for a widow with two children to manage. Kate was pleased with her mother's decision to come to Seahurst. She had fallen in love with the wildness of that first winter having known only its soft searing days. What she had found was a challenging enemy of elements; winds that tore the spume from the sea scudding it across the sands like ponies; wind that tore the skin from one's lips should they be licked for the saltiness. Giant sand-packed combers crashed on the beaches. Once she dived under too slowly and she was thrown about as if she were a rag in a huge washer. The combination of sand and broken shells had raked her leg until it bled and it was painfully wrenched. She jumped to the next rock feeling the twinge.

It was here on this jetty that she had seen the greatest array of ships for it was opposite the rendezvous for the convoys. John Masefield's "dirty British coaster with salt-caked smoke-stack" loaded low into the Atlantic; freighters, tankers taken from all the derelict ports of the world pointing a matchstick at the sky, the lone stern gun for protection — they were all here. Except during storms, the sky was not where the foe hid. The U-boats were under their keels and it was not until the blimps were flown in from Lakehurst, nose-diving and dropping their depth charges that the ships got more relief. The destroyers were there camouflaged in crazy designs of black and white and gray. They yelped their sirens as they veered in rippling circles about the ships great and small that were to carry the material to England, or to that death-stretch, the Murmansk run to Archangel.

"Kate O'Reilly, C'est Moi"

"Do you need something for the pain?" She opened her eyes to the soft voice. The face of a girl with black cropped hair was in her line of vision.

"Later," she answered, slipping back to that other place where she jumped to the next rock. "I want to see them before they are gone."

It confused her for the ships were gone. The war had been over for thirty years. The whales in the Gulf Stream were what drove her top speed over the rocks. She would have to be careful now as the waves boomed against the jetty, shafting the air with rainbows. Her footing was not secure. There, there to the north a geyser from an uprising gray body; she caught the image just as three other whales partially submerged. How could they kill them, slaughter them as the U-boats had methodically picked off the strays of the convoys? Oil, ambergris, blubber, whale-bone. Melville, Dana, and countless other writers had not only sailed after them but described their hunts. Now the lamps of China were not supplied by a crew such as Captain Ahab's. She thought of the men who had climbed the riggings of those sailing ships; the clippers racing westward with lead-lined tea chests which made the seas of the world seem safer than traveling on the Freeways. And what of the men who had slipped off icy spars, falling from tall masts, the dirge of the winds their last sounds as they crashed into valleys of the sea? Their deaths were not always noticed for the man working by his side might have been engulfed in a slashing sail.

She knew the dip near the end of the jetty was already washed with waves but if she was careful she could get across the seaweed covered rocks. The leg was almost well. There was no sense in hurting it again just to look at the school of whales. The word, "just", brought a flood of other memories and a smile to her face.

Her family referred to him as Uncle Just, a distant cousin or someone on her father's side, the naval tradition side. His habit was to start a conversation with, "Just a few miles east of Palmer Peninsular..." or, "Just north of Charcot Island where we lost Evans and Nelson..." then he would pull out of his pocket a small atlas and with nicotined finger point out the place in the Antarctic. The family would gather around the kitchen table, have their ritual cups of coffee when he began the tale of his adventures. Four times he had sailed to the South Pole, as well as many other places, then to Spitzbergen, then north with Admiral Byrd. Paul Scope, Uncle Just, had that ability to draw people around him. Kate, and her brother Ted, his girlfriend, Rosemary, listened by the hour. "Just happened to have a slop bucket and not having tested from which direction the wind was blowing..." and he would have them laughing about all the contents drenching him, fighting off imaginary pieces of garbage, wrinkling up his nose which exaggerated a small scar running nor'-east, as he put it, giving him a devilish grin. He could have them laughing one minute, then his mood would change like a shift in the wind, frightening them about how the masts of the ships held the dancing St. Elmo's fires, or how the shadows of leviathans crisscrossed their bows. Once, with tears streaming down his face he told the children (those in the neighborhood had accumulated like barnacles on a hull) how Margaret O'Reilly (her own mother) had thrown out his walrus-skin parka and seal-skin mukluks. "Maggie said they had vermin crawling all over them," he cried, "vermin. I had worn those precious garments, and they had saved my life many a time. I wore them on Scott's first expedition in 1901." His tears were genuine. Children live closest to tears so that made him very special to them for that was their kind of world. Kate really never knew what became of him.

She saw white caps out where the gulf and the Atlantic met. A song her mother used to sing her asleep with began in her head: ..."and every little wave had its nightcap on, its nightcap, whitecap, nightcap on..." That song was part of the naval tradition too — and tea chests with hand painted women in kimonos, Fujiyama looking behind the tea plants; Japanese ceremonial sake bowls imprinted with rice grains; swords and guns, ship's bells, barometers she had kept. "You're nothing but a pack-rat, Maggie," Jim had once scoffed.

For the taking of all the exotic trivia from the sea, certain exchanges had been made. Grandfather Jeremy Blake had caught pneumonia off Greenland and was buried in its green ice waters; an uncle went singing about "Remember the 'Maine'!" and he died as a marine south-west of Santiago at Baiquiri; Kate's cousin, Harold Bellamy, the blacksheep of the family, had not made it out of his Flying Footlocker of a B-24 somewhere off Italy, but he kept to tradition by crash-landing in the Mediterranean.

Ouch. The twinge in her leg was getting worse. Kate thought she heard the cry from behind but when she turned there was just fog hugging the seawall looking as it had for all time, a barrier which could in no way defend Seahurst against the enemy.

Where was the enemy now? The last drifting burning oil had claimed all its victims including the one she had thought was part of a rubber liferaft wedged into the jetty. She saw them on her first day on the job as combination life-guard and swimming instructor, a job she got because all the eligible young men had enlisted or were drafted. The old Scot who ran the club had given her a chance to prove herself, and so she was sweeping the beach clear of seaweed, shells, driftwood, grapefruit rinds, when she came upon what she thought was the raft. It lay collapsed, gripped by the jetty. She tugged, fell backward holding the black oil-soaked arm of a corpse which had slid off as easily as the skin off rotten fruit. Her footsteps, one clear straight line, had led her to the telphone to notify the Coast Guard. Not until her bed that night had rocked like a ship in a hurricane did she think of the man who had been wedged in the rocks, then she had vomited as if she could disgorge all the ships she had seen burning off the beaches, and all the fins of sharks feasting, for war was a feast for them. She could hear the detonations of depth charges from ships and blimps which brought more bloated bodies, along with sea creatures, when the tides changed. And the man, what of the man? Who was he, German, or one of ours? Did it make a difference, the death of one man when there were so many? That question would return to haunt her when she got to college that fall because the world continued its fighting, its slaughter. She turned the question into what difference did it make to be a student in a time of such turmoil? Did it have to make a difference? All the winds from all the places of the world, all the waves seemingly to converge on Seahurst like the convoys, and the whales in the Gulf Stream must have had some meaning. A man meant something. Later, the figure of the six million dead Jews seemed no more mind-blasting than the death of the corpse. Each man has his own meaning.

The leg ached, made thinking hard, distracted her just as logic would if one were caught in riptides where no direction to escape is possible. There would be frantic heaving of one's body to stay abreast of the waves, now slaps in the face, now the peak of a mountain about to come crashing down and the word *drown* was too soft or innocent for such a dying. Once she had been carried out to sea for almost a mile before she could drift near the edge then break through the current to make it back to shore.

Looking out now, she saw that the whales were gone. There was that slight variation of color between the Gulf Stream and the Atlantic. The water spouts had moved north as the great mammals continued their migration, now as forever, they swam north to south, then south to north, carrying with them the lore of the sea. And they were gone. She was very tired. She would like to stay here on the rock and smell the salt water, taste it on her lips like tears. Surely there were not tears for the sight in front of her was a beautiful swelling sea, clear blue sky with no insect-winged aircraft surveying. The sea was playing at being a friend. The monsters were hidden below while only a jellyfish waited to jab as a reminder that it too had its wrath, its value of life.

She felt a sting on her thigh.

"There, that injection ought to help you rest easier," the nurse said withdrawing the needle.

Her body felt cold. The pain in her left foot was subsiding as the muscles seemed to relax. She opened her eyes and saw ice rise and fall while off in the distance a mountain rose. Hail strong enough to skin a rabbit was hitting the glass window. Strange how the mountain loomed above the storm clouds. Was it Erebus, or Mt. Terror, named after the ships of James Ross in 1841? In "The Race to the South Pole", she had found many of the places, men and ships Uncle Just had written about in his journal. Here she felt at home, a place to go where no one could find her, or touch her. A wall of ice protected her. More so than the people who had come in to see her and who seemed embarrassed by what was happening. Perhaps only one person understood what she was going through. He came three or four times a week, never staying long, but his presence was healing. His gift of books seemed priceless. If only she could write as in the book he had given her, in that lyrical declarative truth about the brave men out there on the ice. Other men did follow in their steps. His book, and the journal of Uncle Just were a lodestone for survival, passed from man to man in much the same way the whales passed on their traditions. So much depended upon responsibility. Then she thought of the Siberian ponies that Uncle Just had fed on the ship and it bothered her, and the dogs too. She always loved animals, and these had to be considered as different, as transportation and food rather than for companionship. Ernest Shackleton had gone to slaughter

83

"Kate O'Reilly, C'est Moi"

houses in England before he sailed south into that ice-bound continent in order that he might rid himself of his aversion to the sight of animals being slaughtered.

She shivered and drew the blanket higher about her shoulders. The lonely howl of the wind added to the sound of the hail striking the windows. The left leg was heavy although the spasms had stopped. She closed her eyes again wishing for a mug of steaming cocoa that the explorers drank in their tents, seeking the warmth of a sleeping bag, desperately wanting sunshine. Try to think of something green, green, she repeated. Try to think of the tree farm where she had worked on and off for the past twenty years.

The trees were green and beautiful. She did her writing in the mornings and in the afternoons had gone over to the plantation working with her friends Irene and Charles Whitcomb. He had been one of her professors at the New England college. Of the sixty-thousand pines, spruces, firs, she wondered just how many she had started on their way? That first spring she road a roan, a lanky horse who plodded higher and higher on the mountain side to the lot where they had put in the first yearling trees.

"Watch that 'Rusty' doesn't step in a chuck hole or he'll probably break a leg." Whitcomb reminded her. The currents of time carried her back. Her legs gripped his flanks in order to stay on and she held his head high. The canvas sacks dripped water from the seedlings. When Charles Whitcomb got to the boundary stakes, they dismounted and got out their spades and shovels. The earth was black and soon the routine of digging holes, getting the young roots down securely, covering them and watering them went quickly. A tabulator kept track of how many went into the long rows running parallel to the mountain. They did not seem hardy enough to survive the wind that blew in April but a soaring hawk caught the golden sunshine as if reflecting it down to the young trees where someday his brood would hunt.

In winter the trees made mounds under the snow which as the years passed outshot their igloos revealing their bright green boughs. It was hard work, physically tiring, just the thing to clear the mind after the writing. She enjoyed being out in the four seasons which are part of New England. The shore she had left seemed comprised of either scorching heat, or north-easters with their bone-chilling cold. The Fourth of July races signalled all the young to the beach club striving for the various medals to be won. Her own, won over the years, had made her eligible for the job at the pool. When she had gone away to college, to the mountains, she became homesick until one evening the mists rising off the fields seemed a peaceful anchorage in the valley, a safe harbor where the lights of the town twinkled below and no sailor need fear a storm. What was missing were the sounds of the sea, the waves, the gulls, the buoys. Here she became haunted by the problem of being a student when the world had gone mad with war.

Charles Whitcomb taught creative writing and he found in this student a spiritual desolation, a striving loneliness which found release through words. He encouraged her, "But remember," he told her, "to go on you must find part time jobs to sustain your writing. Don't forget that." She began working in the college library finding a sense of well-being surrounded by the stacks, compatible with what she jokingly referred to as her navy tradition character.

Her mother died hitting a bridge abutment in a Jersey fog during her freshman year. She could not cry. No tears came. The funeral was a pantomime.

Ted graduated from high school three months later but she did not even return. She had received a letter from her brother saying he had enlisted and was serving on a cruiser in the South Pacific.

"What the hell good is it to be a writer sitting on an ivory mountain overlooking a peaceful anchorage when a war rages?" she questioned Charles Whitcomb. No tears, only anger because home also had been wiped away with her mother's death. And he tried to tell her to read. "Read, and read during these times when you can't write because believe me for every word written you must fill yourself with a million. You must have as many words and thoughts as there are stars, or," and he had put his arm on her shoulder feeling her withdraw, "our trees." Only then did one tear fall. She liked it that he credited her also with the planting of what was becoming a successful business where many people came to select their own Christmas tree. During the holidays she donned jeans, parka and insulated boots to go saw down her tree, drag it for what seemed miles across the snow to the farm. The cold air was like the songs Uncle Just had taught her; even without the sea, the cold winds carried the messages of whales and dolphins, penguins, the Siberian ponies whose small hoofs could not save them from tumbling into crevasses, blue-green fissures opened under their weight, sometimes dragging a man down with them. Shackleton had had a pony named "Socks" and she thought if ever she were to have a dog she would name him after that pony.

In the hospital she had a recurring nightmare where "Socks" had fallen into a crevasse. He struggled to get some kind of footing against the ice which kept cracking under him. He neighed. She lowered herself down by ropes only to have them slip. His terror became her own. The nightmare always ended with her slipping further down from the rope and the pony neighing in her ears.

That last summer on the Jersey shore she met a man, an Englishman from the naval hospital and they had corresponded when she was at college. On leave, he had come up to see her. They had spent his two weeks furlough together on Cape Cod in an old inn where apple logs blazed on the grate. They had talked as if there would be a tomorrow. It was as natural to follow him to his bed as if forever they would remain side by side through the years ahead. When he sailed off on a North Atlantic patrol, his letters reiterated those feelings. Her work took on an additional intensity for she now spoke in the language of her heart and there were people who sometimes never find another to speak it to. She was even in love with his name, Sub-Lieutenant Peter Holmes, and the name of his ship, H.M.S.

"Pursuer", Royal Navy. She sent him her crude strivings for stories and the one that got published for twenty-five dollars. With part of the money she bought him a record of Bing Crosby singing, "Don't Fence Me In". Their joke was that he had a girl in Glasgow, one in Alexandria. He loved the American west, seeing out there, from books and films, all the beauty and mystery she received from the oceans of the world. "The good die young, Kate," he had written in a letter which came bound in a packet with the censors' tapes across the bottoms. And then it became true. There were no more letters from him. She died in her heart, filled with eons of darkness, despair without tears became as part of her backbone. She tried digging herself into her writing as if she would send it to him when she had finished. Rosemary announced her engagement, but not to Ted; others around her were getting married, inevitably the children began arriving. She left college after three years without a degree for she did not feel it important to be a student with Peter dead. The question which had tormented her resolved itself. Life was simple after all.

She found a house surrounded by woods near a small pond which became a token for the sea where Peter Holmes lay forever without her.

An anthropoligist from the college hired her to help him with a research problem. She covered sheets in ledgers about small towns in the mid-west, charts on incomes, jobs, unemployment, birth rates, mortality rates, and at night, if she had the energy, she wrote.

Her love went out to small creatures: rabbits, racoons, possums who were so ugly and shy that she could not resist feeding them. The birds she learned by species and their songs. She bought a Chesapeake retriever whom she named "Socks". The children in the village loved him too for his soft cocoa colored wool, a grinning bear, he would chase their balls and remember each child with his pink tongue. After fourteen years of devotion she had chiseled his dates on a small marble slab placed above the grave near where the stream met the edge of the woods.

The girl in white stood suddenly at her bedside. "Ready for your lunch?" The tray held baked chicken, string beans, salad and fruit. They were taking good care of her. Sometimes there was pain. In fact, Kate had complained that it was the other girl in the next bed who was moaning and in a strange voice the nurse had quietly said that her room was a private one. It was the other girl who watched the flukes of whales plunging in the Gulf Stream off the jetty; that other girl who had lived on the supply ship in the Antarctic, and who slept loveless in New England since her youth had gone. In the tradition of the navy, her family, the whales, the songs of her life had become silent, evident only by the filing cabinets of short stories and rejection slips, thousands of them it seemed. At one time she had thumb tacked them to her study wall before they ground her writing to a halt.

The doctor opening the door brought in a cold draft of air. He was middle aged with long blond hair to the collar of brown corduroy. Tired lines accentuated his eye sockets and the corners of his mouth. He was saying, "We tried to stop the spread of the infection, but now it seems we will have to operate after all."

She could not speak from the shock of his statement. His eyes were pale blue. Why, she wanted to ask him, yet she had known all the time that it was gangrene. Surely she had read enough about Jones and Henderson in the journal, and in "The Race to the South Pole" to recognize the symptoms. Why had it taken them so long?

Thinking of her toe, black as the arm she had pulled off that corpse in the jetty, she gave a diagnosis herself. "The toe must come off."

The doctor shook his head then swept back a lock of hair which had fallen over his eyes. "No, it's gone too far for that."

The nurses had been swabbing her with twelve inch cotton probes from one side of the foot to the other and halfway up to her knee. She always pretended that it did not bother her, no, they were not hurting her.

"At my ankle?" She wished she knew how to handle herself. His eyes blinked once. "No, closer to the knee."

Inside her head she heard the echoes of "Sock's" neighing in the crevasse and she wanted to scream for the indignities of having lain chained to I-Vs, dependent upon hypodermics, and barrages of tests, and insulin shocks as if she had been kicked in the stomach by one of the Siberian ponies. With the shocks followed the sensation of starvation. Uncle Just's journal had recorded the dreams of the men starving out on the polar ice and their reactions held the same mad cravings for food although she was not suffering from malnutrition. Hers, the trickery of diabetes. When she thought of all the consultations, the pages of caloric intake, output of vital fluids, why could not this infection have been halted by the minutiae of routine? She fell silently back into that white land where she had been hiding from all of them since she had entered the hospital. There was only one person she longed to see, her friend who had given her the books. He understood about alien terrain. The answers lay in the books, and in what that other woman would always remember about the war.

We'll do the amputation Thursday. Dr. Bradley is an excellent surgeon. We're not anticipating any trouble." When she said nothing, he removed his hand from the raised footboard. "I'll be in to check with you later." No sooner was he out the door when a girl entered.

She was tall and also blonde, a student, for she wore the yellow uniform which distinguished them from the veterans in white. There was no energy left in Kate to respond with speech or smile. The coldness in her was marrow deep and she thought she heard a dog howl, or was it the wind whipping about? Then softly as the waves washing a beach at low tide, the girl was asking her for permission to go into the operating room in the morning. Kate shuddered thinking of how the arm had come off the corpse. She studied the face of the girl.

"If I understand what you feel, what you go through..." she bit her lower lip, "well, I might become a better nurse." Kate nodded. "I shall stay right at your side. You look so tired. Try to get as much rest as you can. And thank you."

89

"Kate O'Reilly, C'est Moi"

The white ridge heading toward Mt. Terror stretched beyond the sheets. The ponies had all died out there, as had the men, if not then and there, later. For her heroes were Scott and Shackleton, and the one man, Peter Holmes, she had been able to open to. Other women went from man to man, it was in songs how love is a game and people were interchangeable. I am not, Kate told herself, and a sharp stab of anger ran upward from her belly. "I will not be complete, not if they amputate." Except for this furious moment she had not reacted. Room 794 was a bed, clean linen, thermometers, bedpans, and food trays, water jugs, and smiles; once in a while a silent nurse obviously worried about something before or after this case. Objectivity was the oil that made the wheels run smoothly. Was she really part of that navy tradition which gave so generously of its men? What about women? "It's taken you more than half your life to come to this important question, Katherine." The voice was unmistakenly that of her mother. There was something to be realized by way of courage but she wondered how to achieve that.

She knew her friend who had brought her the books and who had never failed to visit her had given her part of the answer by his being steadfast. He never wavered. In those books she knew she was trying to learn how to handle herself with dignity. In dreams she could escape from reality; it helped remembering the jetty where she could think of Peter Holmes, search for whales, and soak up the sunshine and the windsting.

The leg was so bad that she could not have even attempted to run away. The morning of the operation, Fay, the student nurse, came early and held her hand as she was swept by waves of nausea, diarrhea which finally stopped when an injection was administered. Her eyelids were so heavy she could not open them. Fay held her hand as they wheeled her down the hall to surgery. Robert Scott had written in his diary before he died, "For God's sake, take care of our people." She felt herself to be in that dark, cold, snapping tent where they had found him, and she kept repeating those words as a prayer. Then they amputated the leg.

Time lost whatever meaning it ever had. The minutes did not tick off into hours, or days but sped like lightning or else dragged backward. One night she lay with Peter in the rose wallpapered room of the inn and he held her against himself to calm the tremors, not speaking, and she knew from this that he was dead, yet she felt him stroking her hair, her face, and she lifted herself to him to receive all that he could give her, crying, knowing there was nothing left in her to give him but pain. Then she was swimming under water past an ocean trough where in murky gloom, half-buried in sand, his carrier swayed with the currents. Time no longer held any true meaning for her.

In the Physical Therapy room she exercised, tried balancing first on a walker, then crutches with a wide leather belt in order to remain upright, fearing every moment that she would fall into a crevasse. Her body did not know how to move with the leg gone. In her room there were times when she forgot and she would put down what they referred to as the "phantom leg". The rude awakening pain as she hit the floor reminded her that a new leg would never grow; her resolve not to remain forever being tended helped her back to her crutches to try again. She must learn to march to the tune of a prosthesis. The cost of these past three months was far above her income for the next three years and she had to depend on what the health insurance would pay.

The hospital was more than generous. "When you get out and settled," the social worker told her, "then you come in and we'll discuss how best to handle your situation. The main thing is for you to get well and on your feet," and she had looked down at her own where the bed held a depression on the left side. "Now don't worry."

"Thank you," Kate said. It meant so much to her — what everyone in the hospital was doing and it was so little to say for all who had cared for her, a stranger in an alien land.

The last skirmish was the beginning of a war. "The boot" as she referred to the prosthesis would cost in the neighborhood of thousand dollars. This figure loomed astronomically high as the galaxy of the Milky Way. There was no more money. The social worker suggested that she speak with the people of The New England Social and Self-Advancement Association.

One bright sunny day a Miss Rosalie Thorn, a trim ship, her father might have labeled her, for she was as straight as a spar, came in and folded her skirt over her knees as she sat down in the lounge chair with a questionnaire.

"Payments to Social Security seem to have been left out of your earnings," she began. "When did you begin to work and what were some of the jobs you held so that I may have a record of them for our files?"

"I'm a writer," Kate said, "but I've worked since I was seventeen."

"Doing what?" asked Miss Thorn, ball point poised over a sheaf of paper.

The examination of her work began when she told about that first proud day she had become the swimming instructor and life guard. "I also served as an air-raid warden," she added.

"Were you paid by the town?"

"No, it was my volunteer war effort."

Miss Thorn did not find that significant. "And then what did you do?"

College was telescoped, all three years, into a brief sentence about the library job. The depression which followed first the death of her mother, then of Peter Holmes found her withdrawing from part time jobs, not even able to write for long periods of time. What to answer the woman with the poised pen? What had she done with herself if not to write when she could? There were her swimming medals which were good once again for a stint at the Y as an athletic director twice a week, more play than a job. Love did not claim her time. When had she had time for that except on his brief last leave? A voice cried out inside that since she had known him her life was richer, but this was not the kind of information wanted. She told of the anthropological study which lasted a year and a half. She did plant and prune her beautiful evergreens which now were gone. New ones had been replanted as so many had been sold since she had ridden "Rusty" up the mountain. She did drive for an elderly doctor and typed his medical reports, shopped for him and ran all types of errands.

Miss Thorn finally smiled. "Girl Friday," she wrote across the top of the page.

Again the anger about the operation flared to life; being the mute corpse in Room 794 convulsed itself into being. "I am a woman in her fifties. I have had some education." Kate stopped remembering the lonely footsteps on the sand of Robinson Crusoe, the excitement he had when he had found the prints of the other man, the rescuing of the one he named Friday. That long servitude both men shared struck her mind with only one word — slave. She raised herself to face Miss Thorn. "Friday was Robinson Crusoe's slave."

The smile vanished from Miss Thorn's face. She shuffled her forms into a neat stack. "From the description of what jobs you've had I see no other category under which to place you. What vocation do you think you belong under?"

"Writer," said Kate without hesitation. My God, her whole life had been that of a writer. Her litany began: "Thoreau, Melville, Conrad, Henry James, Hemingway, Flaubert..."

"Flo, who?" asked Miss Thorn.

Kate saw Gustave Flaubert bent over his desk staring at the questionnaire. "Not Flo, who. Emma Bovary." He read the question: "Who was Madame Bovary?" and he threw his quill aside shouting, "Madame Bovary, c'est moi!"

"Gustave Flaubert wrote 'Madame Bovary'," said Kate as if that would explain it. She saw that it did not. Poor Flaubert. Yet he had not ground to a halt as Kate O'Reilly had. Along with the medals was the other side of the coin, the files of rejection slips, the white feathers of cowardice. In all those years only two stories published was ridiculous. When she had been sitting in the wheelchair, people had taken to patting her on the head and now this memory fueled her anger as if she was like "Socks", or some other animal. Life had to be more than the wastes of the

Antarctic. Maybe it was her proving ground for this ordeal. "My jobs were part time so that I could write," and she saw Miss Thorn underscore Girl Friday.

It was as if the surgeon had begun the amputation without the anesthesia. "No," yelled Kate, "writer!" She felt the salt tears run down her cheeks, not the salt spray of her beloved sea.

America, the land of the free, and the home of the brave. But there is no anchorage for a writer who is a coward. Robinson Crusoe had cursed the giant combers to preserve his sanity. The cowardice had been hiding in her heart all these years surfacing only on that morning when the operation took place.

"Miss O'Reilly, if you persist in this line," Miss Thorn snapped shut her ballpoint pen, "I'm afraid the committee will find that you are ineligible for the prosthesis. You see we have our guidelines and we have no category to include a writer. Oh," she was distressed when she looked at her wristwatch. "I'm due at a meeting. It will work out, believe me," but her quick look at Kate convinced her that she was being viewed as some bizarre creature. She walked to the door and opened it.

"But Miss Thorn, my writing comes first. I took part time jobs in order that I could write. That's what most of us have to do. Why isn't it listed under a vocation? I don't understand. I don't understand my having to be Girl Friday?"

Miss Thorn smoothed her unwrinkled shirt, shot another look at her watch. "You simply must be Girl Friday you see as we have no category for writer. I've explained all this to you."

Kate could not give up her anger, she would have need of it again. "What I want to know is why isn't a writer a category?"

Miss Thorn had cold evaluating eyes. She dealt with all kinds of requests from all sorts of people but the ritual of her life's commitments defined the realities of every situation she could comprehend. "My dear," the voice was colder than the eyes, "a writer doesn't need a leg." With that remark she closed the door on the wild frigid night where no stars shone, hardly any sun, yet as Kate listened carefully she heard the voices of not only her father, and all the O'Reilly men and women, but Uncle Just, and Peter Holmes, and all those who did not make it on the convoys from all over the world begin to laugh, the laughter turning into the song of the whales and the wind. She would walk out of this place knowing that still the fear was in her, that she would fall, but that she would leave footsteps on the sand on some beach some other day.

That Certain Glow VIII

If there was one thing in life that Bill McGonigle loved it was a good fire. He lifted the lid off the kitchen stove, stirring the ashes to uncover the glowing embers. Carefully he waited for the kindling to catch before he fed in the first chunks of wood. Even if the cost of power had not gone sky high Bill McGonigle would not have abandoned their old kitchen range which burned either wood or coal. He had grown up with its steady warmth; now he mostly burned wood because the railroad had taken off its coal spur from New York State. The freight yard did not know where or when any future coal deliveries could be made.

Bill figured that he had enough coal left to last them from this spring until mid-winter. At seventy-eight he was slowing up. The arthritis in his legs kept him from walking out of his hollow to forage for wood on the border of Luther Robinson's property.

Mag, his sister, was two years his junior. Since her stroke last year she was confined in the house and depended upon her brother more than on her husband Ted, or Trap as he was called by the village who remembered him from boyhood carrying steel-jawed traps, and the dead creatures he had caught. Trap had served a year during World War I in a boot camp never leaving the New Jersey fort where he had been stationed. Once when the train bearing Calvin Coolidge had stopped at the railroad station he had stood at attention in a small line of veterans and the president had shaken his hand. It was his proudest memory. Trap helped run the house, but it was up to Bill to tend the fires.

This damp morning made Bill's legs ache. There was no way he could make it to the Robinson land for wood and only a few weeks ago Luther had shouted down to him as he sat on the porch: " 'Good fences make good neighbors.' Robert Frost." On the other side of the fence was a good supply of oak, birches, and maples.

This thought gave his mouth a bitter taste, for over fifty years he had been subject to Luther's quotations, poetry and Biblical and disparaging remarks about his Church of St. Francis, about the many priests who had served there. Old Bill could not remember all the priests he had seen come and go. There was something about this Vermont village which made for good priests and this thought soothed him as he reached for the skillet to begin breakfast.

He was the first up when the birds began to sing, stirring himself awake in the low ceilinged bedroom and dreading to pull off the covers for that first splash of cold air. Spring, summer, fall, winter that old house being in the hollow was always damp. When it was cold he would undress downstairs over the furnace grate, often leaving his clothes there until morning.

His first chore would be to tend the coal furnace in the basement, clinking, clanking it to burn; the ashes he would carry up with him to leave on the back porch where later Trap got them to put behind the barn. He burned wood in the kitchen stove and started the day with a pot of green tea, Mag was partial to the green. The slab of bacon was sliced thick, sizzled from long chunks to small black squares. Into the deep grease he would break one egg for Mag, two for himself, and three for Trap. By the time the tea was brewed in the pot that his mother had brought with her from the old country, he had the bread on the wire racks over the flame tamer, a plate he sometimes forgot to put over the fire so that on those mornings Trap, the next one down, would have to open the windows and doors of the kitchen to rid it of the heavy smoke. Dutifully Bill would scrape the burnt toast: "a touch of charcoal is good for the stomach," he would say, and Trap usually gave him that sour look on his thin face which seemed reserved for most of the things old Bill said. Bill had taken to silence over the past thirty years since his sister had married. Still the three of them had managed to keep their home, run down as it was getting to be, and remain free from the gaily decorated nursing home smelling of urine he had once visited fifty miles away. That was the time Mag had dislocated her shoulder and some "young know-nothing of a doctor" as Trap had called him, wanted them to commit her. "But Mr. Ahern, she would be well looked after. I don't see how you and your brother-in-law can manage. There is an occupational therapy room with basket making, weaving, a library and a large color TV." How the three of them had winced. They got up at five a.m., each lived his own life, and were in bed by eight p.m. Who had time for TV? Who wanted TV? Surely not the Ahearns and McGonigle.

Outside the kitchen windows facing the Robinson ridge, the garden was ruled by weeds. Once in a while a boy was hired to cut the grass which made it resemble an empty lot. The rose trellis and grape arbor were gone. Mag used to ask about her flowers before her stroke when her eyes got so weak. "Are the scylla up?" Bill knew the small bright blue flowers bordering their porch which she fancied. His sister knew what grew on their land. Few he recognized.

"What do you mean by those yellow headed bloody weeds?" she asked when he described pulling out these strangling weeds from the lily of the valley. The lilacs had eventually overshaded her swamp pinks.

"Your wandering Jew had wandered away," Trap had told her one day for in its place grew mouse's ear. The snakes had stayed leaving their skins as reminders.

Her sweet peas had been the pride of Deepdale Street as were her three shades of morning glories, her peonies, the lemon and tiger lilies. She had once grown tulips which were almost black but Bill looking out of the window could find no trace of them.

The garden used to seem eternal for as soon as one species faded another sprang into bloom.

The old apple tree still grew crooked with now only worm-eaten fruit falling from its upper branches. A long time ago, Mag had rushed in, her face like a bride's to tell them that she had seen twelve ruby-throated hummingbirds circling above the sweet white blossoms, a crown of hummingbirds. One night she had seen the fire flies dancing in a huge silver circle against the stars of Orion's belt and sword.

"No wonder you burn the damn toast, and eggs, and bacon what with you always staring out of the windows," Trap said startling him out of the past. "How long before we eat?" He washed his hands for he had been getting Mag up from her bed where she slept in what had been the front parlor. She was sitting in her rocking chair listening to the radio. The day would be one of dozing and waking, living in and out of past, everyday.

"Can you see what Luther Robinson has been up to? Heard all kinds of racket these past few weeks." Trap was as lean as his brother-in-law was fat. He pulled aside the green checkered curtain to look to the east.

Although Luther Robinson kept his front lawns on East Street looking neat, he had let the back lot remain a meadow just as it had been when his father, the banker, had kept a herd of Herefords. At the border of their property Luther used to wheel cart loads of trash, garbage, which he dumped where it was visible when the leaves were off the trees and which smelled when the wind blew from that direction. The crown-insult, even beyond the fence, had been when Luther had ordered six headstones years ago at a special price and when he had had an argument with one of the family, he had taken one of the stones in his wagon to dump on the pile where it ended up leaning against the wires, the name ROBINSON plainly visible.

"Damn headstone staring us in the face every day of lives," Trap snorted as he shoved the curtains together. "Hurry up with

Mag's tea. She's feeling poorly these damp spring mornings. And when are you going to do something about the weedpatch so you can start growing us some vegetables?"

"Today," old Bill said, preparing the tray for his sister, careful not to forget the little pot of honey she liked on her toast and in her tea. "That brush grass has got to go. Why don't you ever lend me a hand?" It was a helpless appeal for it was not the plan of Trap's life to be concerned with the land, except for the times he had been concerned with the creatures that lived on it.

In the past the shot gun had always stood loaded by his rocking chair on the porch and he had picked off his fair share of rabbits, woodchucks, skunks, possums. Once he had killed a family of racoons, the darker male laid beside the lighter colored female, the three kits frozen in death alongside. For years he had kept the barn with crows nailed from wing to wing, or chicken-hawks and owls. He liked to walk to the post office each morning to talk about the good old days, stopping at the Drink & Think, half the room filled with the long time residents, the other with the new people. With his coffee he would roll himself a Bull Durham cigarette and sit till late morning before returning home to snooze on the porch before dinner. The Standard arrived about two; they would eat an early supper, stacked dishes washed, and the day was done by eight p.m.. Life was simple, uncomplicated for Trap Ahearn.

The McConigles were a different breed; the trivialities comprised a continuing story as sister and brother made a preciously woven cloth from their childhood memories, a bridge from the past to each new day.

Bill watched until Trap brought in the tray. He stacked the dishes in the sink where they would sit, the cigarette butts congealed in grease; flakes of tea leaves sprinkled over all until after their evening supper at five. Then the two men sloshed away at them, and they were left to drain.

"Better put your sweater under your jacket," Trap suggested, "mean wind out. Got any matches?"

Bill took a handful of wooden ones from the table beside the stove to stick in his pocket.

"You dropped three," said Trap, knowing how difficult it was for him to bend over but he just stood there so Trap grunted and picked them up to put with the others.

"Thanks," Bill muttered. His mother's voice came clearly to him: "The Irish always fight among themselves. Pay no mind. Save the fighting for outsiders."

He stepped onto the rickety stoop thinking that Trap should fix it one of these days. A blue jay went screaming toward Mt. Abraham. The wind was blowing down from Robinson's ridge and would carry the flames across the garden. From the side of the porch he took a rake, walked the path worn clean from the comings and goings of the creatures who were no longer shot at and who had come back to this land. Their house was built in the middle of an acre but was only fifty feet from the hated fence. The other two sides had trees shielding them from the sight of their neighbors.

The long yellow grass did not start for the dew clung in rainbows, so Bill slowly returned to the porch where the Standards were stacked. Making newspaper balls he was able to start a fire, made a few sweeps with the rake and stood back to watch. A gust of wind from the opposite direction swept his hat off which he retrieved with the rake, grunting as he put it back on. He could see the lace curtains rippling where he knew Trap was watching. The land was not his to care for, Trap had made that quite clear. Repairs to the house, shopping, those were his domain.

A catbird scolded as the smoke began rising and Bill hurried to keep the sparks from spreading in the wind. The fire was mushrooming up the rise. He took off his jacket, then his sweater feeling the heat from the burning field. If he could have moved faster he would have seen the flames had already passed the fence and were nibbling at the base of the trash pile. From there it seared rapidly to the rows of the young spruces which Luther Robinson had been planting.

By the time the fire trucks arrived Bill McGonigle had not only burned his upper lot, (Trap had saved their porch by dowsing it with buckets of water and shoveling), but he had killed all the spruces.

A meeting was called at the fire house that evening by Chief Chet Cummings. He asked why McGonigle had not phoned that the fire was out of control immediately but old Bill had not realized that the dump had caught fire, besides he was ashamed to admit that he could not get up the rise, and that they had no telephone.

"Damn it, Bill," Chet said, "you did a fair amount of damage to Robinson. If he hadn't called he might have lost his house, not to mention some others on East Street."

Bill sat at the long table with Trap at his side, rubbing his smoke-streaked eyes, and feeling his parched throat.

Luther Robinson stood up. He was a small man in his sixties standing on the balls of his feet like a boxer. "I hollered at the idiot but it did no good. My trees..." he spluttered, "who pays me for my trees, my work? You?" he pointed his finger at the two men he hated. "Didn't have the brains to call the fire department. Had to do that myself."

Chet Cummings rapped for silence and Robinson sat. Carefully he pieced the story together. Robinson was asking for a large sum of money for his trees. Bill and Trap sat quietly in defeat. They had not a fire permit and that carried a fine of fifteen dollars.

Keeping a large brush pile within the village constituted a fire hazard.

"No way was that a compost heap." Cummings ruled that Luther Robinson was guilty but that he would suspend the fine as he had suffered enough by the financial loss of his trees.

He turned to Bill and Trap. "You should have had a permit." Bill knew that Trap drank coffee every morning with Chet and the whole village knew of the fencing off of the land, and the tombstone looming like a miniature Mt. Rushmore with the Robinson name instead of a face.

"I'm going to suspend your fifteen dollar fine this time too." Robinson jumped to his feet. "Sit down, Luther. The garbage heap was bad enough but I want you to put that damn headstone somewhere else." He turned back to the two older men. "Next time you decide to burn something get a permit and have a boy help you. Case closed."

Bill saw Robinson going downstairs, his thick yellow-white hair cut across the back the way his mother had done when she used a bowl to keep it even. Once the brick red face of his neighbor glanced back at him. "There is something that doesn't love a wall," Bill was tempted to quote another part of the Robert Frost poem.

The following evening supper was a cold one at the old people's house. When the sun went down the chill set in.

"Where's my tea?" snapped Mag. "Bill didn't make me my tea. One can't have a decent meal without tea."

Trap finally had to make it for old Bill sat dejectedly in his rocking chair; the Standard on the floor where he had let it fall. That day he would have no part in tending to the furnace or the kitchen stove. He, who as a boy used to watch his father, the blacksmith pound the orange horseshoe to the shape of the hoof, sparks flying when the hammer struck; the sizzling as he dipped it, then fitted it to the horse. His father used to make him rings out of the nails. Masie O'Neal wore one a whole summer before she turned her sixteen year old smile on Oliver Townsend. He sought refuge in the past before the time of Luther Robinson and his hated fence. He thought of the houses he had spent his life painting and unlike most who complained of the harshness of the paint fumes upon their throats, did not turn to drink for relief. He provided for himself and his sister even after she had married Trap. He had never married. Of love he thought he understood nothing, nor how Mag could share her life with a man who trapped and hunted. When the spirit moved Trap, as he put it, he had done a few odd jobs, carpentry, deliveries, that kind of work. Bill knew himself to be an old man, the fire confirmed it; an old arthritic man whose life seemed to be as devastated as the land he had sought to make green.

"Oh, hell, Bill," Trap sat down on the frayed horsehair sofa by his side, "so what are a few trees to that bird. Never did a lick of work in his. Lived off Papa, the banker. Played at running a garage he was given." He took out his sack of Bull Durham rolling the coarse tobacco and licking the paper firm. "Got a match?"

Bill saw the gaps in Trap's teeth as he sat grinning at him.

"If you get that sod busted, might even put in a few rows of onion sets for Mag, few tomatoes, beans, or what about some of them sugar peas she fancies?"

Trap was as good as his word for after breakfast he went out and came back from Lampron's Market with a bag of onion sets; at Randolph's Greenhouse he had ordered two dozen tomato plants, three of them the yellow kind which would be delivered later along with a few other vegetables.

Bill could not believe it when he saw Trap spading the soil, turning it over with a fork and mixing the compost he kept behind the barn till the earth looked right for planting.

"You going to sit on the porch all day watching an honest man work?" he asked Bill, and that brought the old man back to the land when he saw the tender green shoots sprouting.

Mag sat listening to her old records still in their original dust-jackets. The music poured forth from a horn-type phonograph. "Trap gave me these Paul Whiteman as a present once," she smiled.

The house kept out the heat of summer as they ate from their vegetable garden. Once a shirkshire storm tore off some slate from the roof, that tornado-like wind which hops and skips destruction where it will. Something about its fury reminded Bill of Luther Robinson's wrath at the firehouse. But his anger must have been passing like the season for they had not heard nor seen anything from him until one autumn morning when Bill was making breakfast he heard the snarl of a chain saw. Trap joined him at the window where they saw a man in a windbreaker on the rise begin to make the saw whine as it bit into a maple just over the fence where the headstone had been. They were speechless when they heard the thundercrack as the great tree swayed and came down heading for their house. Both fully expected the roof to come down with it, but all they heard was the slap of the orange leaves hitting the porch steps.

"Right in our garden, Bill."

Going outside they were in time to see the back of Luther Robinson surveying his handiwork. The tree was now on their land blocking the view like a giant fence.

All day Bill thought of how the slow anger had built itself into this rage, this vengeance for the loss of his spruces. It was not until that evening, after supper when the wind began to blow that he relaxed. He woke Trap who was nodding in sleep beside him on the sofa. The clock ticked slowly on the bookcase. A cricket chirped from the kitchen.

"Trap," he saw his eyes open, "it'll make a good fire," and he grinned as the tip of the maple tapped the porch in the wind as a reminder that it was there.

The Fringed Gentian IX

Pamela Burke had lived in Vermont for fifteen years and not once had she been on the Long Trail. As librarian, she had put special articles about the Trail in the display case in spring, again at foliage season, with helpful tips for hikers. With keen pleasure she found herself one morning in August driving towards the Kelly Stand to meet the others. Wiggling her toes, she felt the snugness of two pairs of socks inside the boots she wore when gardening. Green-dyed Levis, striped cotton shirt with a windbreaker completed her outfit. A neighbor had loaned her a two-quart canteen, and an Army surplus canvas sack which she had filled with some French bread, a slab of store cheese, two oranges and a chocolate bar. She had read that some climbers included sardines, but the early morning weather report forecasted a hot, dry day. Luckily the rain ended the four days of inside living, the clear autumn sun would add an extra joy in going on the trail. She pressed her boot harder on the accelerator to make up for a construction delay outside of Bennington. Two miles east of Arlington, she saw the blue MG waiting at the side of the road. She blew her horn as greeting.

A well-built man in his forties got out of the car and came back to her window. "Good morning," Joseph MacReady said, and she noticed how in the sunlight his hair had white strands in with the black.

"I'm sorry to be late," she apologized, "they were digging up the road. Where are the others?"

At the dinner party where the idea had caught on like wildfire, the Andrews, the Conklins, Joseph MacReady and she had drunk a toast, scheduled to meet up at the Kelly Stand for a five mile hike. "Even a beginner like you ought to be able to do that," Joan Conklin had teased, "you're forty, not fat, but a widow ought to keep in shape."

"Joan told me to wait for your here. We're to take the lower trail, meet them at the firetower. Are you ready?" His handsome face, almost boyish, had a tightness along the jaw which made his annoyance clear. Possible, she thought, he felt her in on a deliberate plot of match-making, a pairing off of the two of them from the others. He need not worry, it was the invitation to the Long Trail which had brought her out of her world of books into the sunshine.

She clipped polaroid glasses over her own. "A perfect day," she said. "If you lead in your car, I'll follow."

He returned to the blue MG, shot up the road with her in pursuit. Joseph MacReady did not drive carefully, she concluded, by the way he spun curves on the wrong side, yet she did not dare to stay too far behind in case he should turn off. Her car bounced and squeaked over the rock-studded road. He flushed a pileated woodpecker from a dead tree, the large bird barely missed flying into her windshield. Had she been alone, she would have stopped to study him at close range. As it was, Joseph MacReady had disappeared around the curve so she had to hurry to keep him in sight. Part-way up the mountain, he stopped, signaled to a cut-off, yelling, "don't go in too far. There's mud."

Deftly she turned in, felt the front wheels easing slightly until she braked. She rolled up the windows, then locked the car although there was nothing in it; it was as clean as when she had bought it second hand the month before.

He waited for her to join him. "Just a few miles more," he said, starting his car again. Some water sloshed out of the canteen onto her thigh. "You haven't got that tight enough," and with one hand he twisted the top. Her shoulder touched his when he swung the car too quickly to avoid a deep rut.

She recognized the Conklin's convertible parked off on the shoulder a short time later. He pulled behind. There was no one around. Checking his watch, he said, "We're twenty minutes late. They must have gone without us."

"I'm sorry," she said which only seemed to irritate him more.

"We'll catch up with them," and a muscle throbbed on the edge of that bold jaw line. He was as determined as she was to begin the hike. "You won't need that," he pointed to her pocketbook, "all the shops are closed." He waited for her to remove a comb, then he stuck the purse behind the seat.

They entered the trail where Pamela stopped to read a sign. "That's for tourists," he said, "come on." She had to catch up with him. The ground was spongy under her boots from the past rain, but the sun was rising above the trees, soon it would burn the ground dry. Patches of milky mist steamed from the meadows. Rain had filled the ruts so she kept to the grassy center behind him, puffing at the rapid pace he moved. She remembered as a girl the familiar second breath, shifting, she used to call it then, when the body adapted for accelerated rhythms, and she waited for the initial panting to wear off. Half an hour later, her breathing was still coming in gasps, the muscles of her right calf were twitching. He had not slowed the pace, so she called ahead, "Do you think we could stop?" The trees grew close together, bushes hid him from her and her boots squelched in mud making the footing difficult. She almost bumped into him.

"We'll take five," he said. Dressed in khaki shirt and trousers, the peaked cap, she felt that a salute would be in keeping with his stance.

"I'll bet you were a drill sergeant," she said.

"Lieutenant," he snapped, his brown eyes meeting her own. She could find not a trace of humor around the corners of eyes or mouth; the glance was dissecting, uninterested.

"And now you will teach economics at the college," Pamela said, thinking how he did not waste breath talking, or time in looking.

"And you are a librarian," he replied. "How are you holding out?"

There was no doubt in her mind that he irritated her and she him. If only Joan Conklin did not insist on matchmaking, they might have started off differently; as it was, they seemed locked in conflict. Briefly he checked the guide book but when she saw him looking at his watch she stood up. "I'm ready."

During the next hour the land became rougher, sometimes the trail was barely visible. They heard the sound of a power-saw whining like some reluctant cat, a displeased panther at their crashing near his lair. Her boots weighed her feet down causing her to stumble. The branches overhead blocked the sunshine; frogs splashed their way in front of her. Sweat trickled down the back of her neck. The sharp smell of Levis, like wet puppy, made her realize that the canteen still leaked. The left hip where it rested was wet. She stopped to see if she could find the leak but the top was on tight. Tracing her hand down to her boots, she felt the dampness. Also the water was heavy but she did not want to pour it out, they might need some. A snapping of wood told her that Joseph MacReady had not waited, so she ran to catch the sight of his boots disappearing in ferns. A blue arrow lay on the trail pointing to the opposite direction.

She heard the water falling long before they reached the ravine. He was sitting on one of the trunks which spanned it waiting for her. He gave her the impression of a model in latest sports fashion, an indifferent gaze protecting him from wind or rain resting there as she staggered up, her feet moving like a toy unwinding with each step.

"Ready?" he asked, getting to his feet. He was barely audible above the rushing water. She peered down to where it ran out of sight, catching the smell of moss, lichens growing on the sides where no sun could penetrate. A breeze sprung the hair on her arm upright, and the perspiration seemed to turn to hoarfrost, as star rays crystallize needle sharp at dawn. She was afraid to cross the log span. Joseph MacReady made his way to the other side but when she put her boot on the log, it slipped off. He turned to see her stepping off the trail to go down a deep cleft.

"What do you think you are doing?" he shouted.

"I'll swim," she yelled back, finding her fingers clutching a fern, root and all, which had given way. her boots struck a rock which kept her from pitching headfirst into the water.

Quickly he recrossed the span, reached to pull her up by the hands. "You can't swim that."

As she regained solid land, they saw a six foot youth coming towards them from the other side. He was followed by a spry, gray haired woman dwarfed by a knapsack. The woman looked up from the trail at them with a face resembling that of the blond giant who was already out of sight. All he carried was a large knife strapped to his waist and a walking stick. With Joseph MacReady and the woman watching her she tested both boots only to feel them slide, and she jumped back. "I can't."

The woman hoisted the pack, adjusted the straps. "Nonsense," she laid loudly, "If I can, anyone can," and she took off after the young man.

Joseph MacReady made no effort to hide his contempt. He checked his watch which added to her nervousness. Then holding out both hands as one does with a child, he said, "Don't look down and take hold."

She looked down to where the water frothed over a toothshaped rock waiting to impale her, but more than ever she felt she must remain free of him. She sat down, straddling the log and felt the seat of the Levis instantly wet on contact as she inched her way over the chasm. He waited for her on the opposite side. Then they trudged on through the woods. After awhile she caught up with him, stopped and brushed the bark from her damp Levis. "When do we meet the others? We've marched for over two hours."

"If we had been on time," he said, "we would have met them at the firetower at nine."

The Fringed Gentian

In all her efforts to keep up with him she realized that she had not seen any birds, or flowers, not even the blue arrows which marked the trail. "Firetower?" she echoed.

"Yes," he said. "Where did you spot our last marker? And by your compass are we heading east?"

The forest screened the sun from her, she could only guess at its position. "I haven't got one," she confessed, "and you travel so quickly, all I see are the heels of your boots."

"My God," he gasped, losing that professional ease, "You hike in the wilderness with no compass? You don't bother to watch for the trail markers? At dinner you gave me the impression you knew all about the Long Trail."

"What's wrong with you?" she said, angry at his attack, "Is your compass magnetized?"

"What compass?" Joseph MacReady's boyishness made him appear quite helpless. "I thought you were the expert hiker."

She began to realize that they were lost and trying to remember the colored threads of trails, the network of paths on the map only made her feel more foolish. "What's that on your waist?" she asked.

"A pedometer. Oh," his dismay increased. "We must have been on a logging trail, missed the firetower. This registers five miles. The whole trip in, and back down to your car should only take that distance. I figured it all out in advance on paper."

She felt an equality at last, on paper they were both experts on hiking. Temporarily Joseph MacReady was still. He squatted silently.

"One thing I learned," she said, "Is to follow water as it always runs down and you'll come out eventually." A spasm of pain in her left leg reminded her of how many miles they had traveled. She listened carefully for the sound of water, some slight trickle, or splashing stream to take them out of here but the whole mountain, at noon, seemed perfectly quiet; no bird call, no wind stirring leaves, only the thick green ceiling they made overhead.

"The loggers must be having lunch," he said, "I don't hear the saw."

"That's a good idea." She pulled the sack around to the front, took out the bread and cheese to hand to him.

"Thank you, no. I never take any lunch. How long will it take you to eat?"

"Five minutes?" and she saw the official nod. With a wolfish bite, she ate the food. The water in the canteen tasted of metal. He rinsed his mouth, spat it out.

"I don't know why you carry that when there is water all around us."

"There is?" she asked, "Where?"

He tapped the book in his breast pocket, "It says there are streams, brooks, lakes." He stood up.

"The book, the book," she said, angry that he was ready to hurry off again, never giving her time to see what lived in this high, wild place. Only from the books had she ever learned anything about the trail. Looking down she noticed a small white blossom growing on a vine. "Oh," she smiled, snapping it off and holding it out to him, "Isn't it lovely. Do you know what it is?"

But he did not take it as a boutonniere, he merely let it fall from his hands. "Some kind of weed," he said. "Ready?"

An hour later she spotted the privy, complete with names, dates, jokes of an elementary nature, a few feet behind a lean-to. Then suddenly, with such beauty she held her breath, she saw the lake opening away from the ridge of pines; so blue and still that it was as if the sky had fallen yet continued to radiate and shine from below. Fire-smudged rocks bordered the water's edge where Joseph MacReady sat for the first time. "Well," he said slowly, "We really did miss them. The stones aren't even warm."

She no longer listened to him but wished she had come prepared to camp for more than a day, or night in the solitude of open space. She imagined what it would be like to cut spruce boughs, sleep under the sky, the smell of a wood fire. The sun dried the shirt on her neck as she took off the canteen, the sack, to lie face upon face to shatter the reflected sky with her lips. There was the taste of earth, of leaves, distilled in rocks in the cool water. She saw the man bent over his guide book, heard him say, "If we bear west we should be able to get back to your car as planned. We can do it in a couple of hours."

The water raised her spirits; two hours were as two minutes and she said cheerfully, "I'm so glad I came. It's beyond what I had pictured. I'm ready when you are."

"Miss Burke, your morale is excellent," he said, standing, "Welcome to the squad."

At the end of the lake, a beaver dam, like wigwam poles stood in the dark water. The path twisted back to the land so uneven and rough she hoped her ankles would not snap like the dead wood underfoot. She heard him call back that he had seen a sign. As she joined him, she saw the board pointing downhill.

"Just another lake," he said, turning away from it.

"I came all this way to see things," she said.

"You just saw one. It's at least two-hundred-twenty feet down."

"I'll walk the extra four-hundred-forty. I'm going to see it."

"A lake's a lake," he muttered, following her to the edge of another clear expanse of blue water.

"How I'd love to go for a swim," she said, feeling the sun beating hot upon her head.

"It's probably full of snakes." He pointed to something gold caught by the sun. "Beer cans. You'd end up by cutting your feet on some broken bottles." He checked his watch. "I wouldn't want to be caught up here after dark."

"I brought matches," Pamela said, wishing for just that chance to camp, to see mountains, the sky melt in darkness, the lake with starlight shining from its mirror. What simple peace it must be to rest one's head and stare straight up at the naked night. She would like to wake, to search for where the Fringed Gentian grew, now rare from being constantly plucked, losing its seed by thoughtlessness. They must be as blue as the water around her. She would have liked to take off her boots pinching her feet, bathe them in the cool water but the man was heading back. She followed behind, waist high in young evergreens on a plateau ringed by dead gray timber. Occasionally her boots stuck logs buried corduroy fashion in the mud from some old road. There were no blaze marks, blue or otherwise in this place he led her. The sun was hot. Their progress was ant-like over the land; she now worried about getting off the mountain. The muscles of both legs were tightening. It would not have surprised her to come face to face with a troop of redcoats, or some of the Ethan Allen boys. Now a dense thicket had them climbing over boulders and fallen trees. It was hard, aching work. "We should sing," she had to pause for breath, "about the bear going over the mountain."

"As long as we don't meet one," his words floated back to her. This wild growth surrounding her on immense scale awed her, the sky and mountains made her keep the sight on his back in view.

At the end of this tangled stretch, the trail sloped down. In her mind she tried to puzzle out the up and down paths, directional changes, labyrinthine ways under tree tunnels. A knotting of both leg muscles slowed her walk and his words, which he had spoken early that morning, "all the shops are closed," made a comprehensible map. "We're heading for my car," she said, unable to check an insane laugh.

Joseph MacReady stopped. Turning around to face her, asked, "What's so funny?"

"All the shops are closed," she repeated helplessly, "My purse is in your car."

"I know that," he said, "I didn't see any point in carrying extra weight. As it is," he looked at the canteen against her hip.

"Don't you understand?" she said, "I locked my car, left the keys in my purse. Oh, what a damned fool I am."

"Very funny, Miss Burke," he said, but her face convinced him that she was not joking. "What kind of thought processes have you anyway? I told you we were hiking back to your car hours ago. What in God's name made you aware of it now?"

The tightening muscles demanded she massage them. "My legs hurt. I'll be all right. I didn't know we had so far to go," she replied, unable to answer his question. "We should get off the mountain before dark," and she began to walk only to have thighs knifed with pain.

"There's a rock ahead," Joseph MacReady said, "Sit down."

The cramps stiffened her legs like wood, then the pain receded.

"I can't move," she said.

"You can," he said, "put one foot in front of the other slowly."

The idea that he might leave her here was frightening; the books had given no truth about the empty stillness, the isolation she felt. Slowly she made her way to the rock. The pain was too intense for her to bend so she leaned against the stone. At his side, she could not help but notice the sharp crease in his trousers although his soaked shirt smelled like beer. "It would take us more than three hours to my car," he said, "Your's is only an hour off."

The tears welled up in her eyes. "I'm such an idiot," she said.

"Eat someting," he suggested. "You can rest by your car and I'll hike back to get mine."

He refused the chocolate but took an orange. The still sky, water and mountains about to turn into a vast darkness made her eat the candy quickly. She put her hand on his arm, glad to be with him, and felt his small movement away from her. Joseph MacReady stood up and his withdrawal restored her pride, her independence. She washed the chocolate down her throat. "All set."

"How could you be? You didn't even masticate the chocolate which takes tens minutes to metabolize."

This odd calculation struck her funny. She could see him before the toaster timing how long it took his toast to pop up at breakfast. A cleft of annoyance between his eyebrows emphasized her determination not to buckle under the cramps in her legs. "Don't tell me," she said, "or I'll stop. Just try a slower pace, Lieutenant," and was glad his efficient figure took the lead.

Lift one boot, it would fall by itself if she concentrated on the other. The land sloped, adding momentum. A blue arrow ahead showed a cleared trail where she recognized the sneaker treads from morning. Not strange at all that they came right out beside her car. She went to both doors pressing the handles in hopes they were not locked. He told her to wait there while he went for his car. She made no protest but sank in exhaustion beside the road. An hour or so later he drove back, handed her the purse without a word. She tried to back out of the ditch but felt the tires dig deeper into soft ruts. He asked her to let him try, but the car was in too deep.

"We'll have to pull you out," he said. "Have you got a chain?"

The trunk revealed nothing but a bag of sand left over from the last owner, and a rusty jack. Joseph MacReady did not carry one either so he went off in what turned out to be a fruitless hour searching for loggers. Once an old truck slowed but by the time she roused herself to ask for help, it had passed. At six o'clock he returned without a chain and suggested he take her down the mountain to a garage. Getting into his car, she felt two bubbles which were blisters open on her heel.

"We were supposed to have had cocktails at five," he said but she did not have the strength to apologize. His indifference made it easy for her to sink into her exhaustion but when she saw the trailer below, she suggested he see if the man there might not pull her out.

A pink shirt, sideburns worn long, and three little girls by his side, the man told Joseph MacReady he could pull her out. "You go ahead to the party," she said, "I'll join you later. I'm sorry to have caused you so much trouble." For the last time she watched the now familiar back as he drove off down the mountain.

The young man drove her back to her car, attached the chain while the children ran in the woods. In a few minutes he had pulled her out, but the chain links had knotted. No matter how he pulled, they remained fast. They had to drive in slow speed back to his trailer where he cut them loose. One of the girls handed her a Fringed Gentian, deep blue, deep as the lakes in that unknown land she had just come from. She gave the children what food she had left, and the man five dollars she had in her purse. Probably if she had asked him how much she owed

117

The Fringed Gentian

he would have tripled the amount, but when she said, "It's all I have," he smiled, gentle with her in muddy boots, wet Levis, the sore leg muscles which had knotted tight as the chain. They would somehow reinforce the knowledge of what it had been like back there on the trail. She would not go to the cocktail party where she was sure Joseph MacReady would tabulate the hours spent hiking, take out his pedometer with the exact number of steps taken to record the distance. Some people are so determined to accomplish life as if it were a blue arrowed trail to be done in so many hours; while others followed, too weak to stop for the reality of the moment. She held the gentian wondering if someday she would ever dare, by herself, return to see if the water was really that incredible blue, or if it only seemed that way now that she had come back down.

A Promise in the Wind X

Phoebe Butler made up her mind to walk to work this morning after seeing the flock of purple finches arrive at the feeder. She told her husband not to wait but asked that he meet here with the car at noon by the Jepson's barn.

"The wind's blowing from the west," Wayne said, looking at the thermometer. "It's only ten degrees."

"To walk will do me good," she said. "Some boys have made a shortcut through the woods. I'll bundle up." She poured the bacon grease into a can, washed the coffee pot for their next meal. Her own housework she did in the afternoons when she had finished cleaning at the faculty houses on campus.

Wayne opened the door, which, caught by the wind, banged against the house. "Winter's going out like a lion," he said. "See you at noon."

She sat down to put on her boots, anxious for the time after the thaw when they could be discarded with the rest of her heavy clothes.

Outside, the air was sharp, the sun not high enough yet to bring much warmth. She followed Pleasant Street down to where their land ended at the fringe of woods, to cut back by the pond at the foot of the campus. The last two days the temperature had been in the forties and she caught a trace of earth-sweetness in the wind. The water ran black in the center of the pond where the ice had broken. She remembered from girlhood how the boys used to stake out the channel, which sometimes froze over. Once she had skated too near, hearing the cracking underneath, but she had gotten away before a section of ice suddenly broke off. With her fifty years, and arthritis, she no longer skated though she enjoyed walking through fields and woods, taking pleasure from all the creatures around. The finches this morning had announced that at last spring had come. Wayne was right though, winter would not go gracefully. She pulled the wool scarf tighter about her ears. Suddenly a shot rang out, a piece of twig fell on her shoulder.

"Heh," she shouted, seeing the two boys silhouetted on the ridge, one still with the rifle poised to shoot. "You nearly hit me." She heard her voice carrying in the clear air. One of the boys swore. The hill must have partly covered her from them, in the thicket, and she realized that her clothing was brown. They were too far off to recognize, just two boys in overalls, olive jackets. Quickly they broke from the ridge. It made her angry that boys always had to shoot at something — a bird, a rabbit. She looked to see what they had been after; only whatever it was had gotten out of sight. Some tracks led to one of the elms farther down. When she had complained to neighbors that boys shouldn't be given guns, they had told her it was because she had no children of her own. "After all, Phoebe," one had said, "it's natural for boys to hunt. Vermont is one of the few places left where folks can grow free." Well, she thought, digging her boots in as she climbed, it's natural, only this land belonged to the college, was posted against hunting and trapping. A few feet more she reached the crest, saw the empty cartridge where the boys had stood. The exertion warmed her, only her face felt the sting of the wind. Below, the pond reflected some blue in its channel. There were no boys in sight. She guessed they were hiding until she passed.

"Good morning, Phoebe," Mrs. Jepson hollered, as she entered the kitchen. "Can you give me a hand? I'm in the bathroom. We've had a little accident." Phoebe walked to where she saw the woman standing naked in the tub, the whole left side of her body streaming with bright red down shoulder, thigh, and into the tub. "I didn't want to stain the floor," Mrs. Jepson said, "so I climbed in here."

Phoebe was so shocked she froze, could not breathe, then fighting for air, she ran to her. "You shouldn't be standing," she said, trying to ease her down. Her hands felt a warm stickiness as she took the sponge to see the nature of the wound.

"Phoebe," Mrs. Jepson said looking at her face, "oh, Phoebe." She laughed. "I'm all right. Norton threw his red finger paint at me."

From the doorway she heard the child giggling, delighted that he had caused further consternation. "Phoebe thought Mummy was killed," he sang. "Phoebe, Phoebe, silly Phoebe thought Mummy was killed." She did not know whether to scold the child first, or the woman, now sitting in front of her laughing. Throwing the sponge in the tub she walked out.

"Seems as how you can best clean that yourself," Phoebe said. "I came to do the housework." She hung her coat in the kitchen still trembling from her shock. Wayne always told her she watched too much TV for her own good, yet the woman had said there had been an accident. Connecting the vacuum cleaner, she did the living room in record-breaking time. Not once did Norton dare unplug the cord, so furiously did she move.

"Norton? Norton?" She heard the mothing calling as she dusted the barn door Charles Jepson had made into a coffee table, each nail hole filled with what seemed putty, but on closer inspection proved to be a cocktail dip, clam from the smell, coated with tobacco ashes. Mr. Jepson taught "Techniques of Art — The Language of Forms" at the college. He was a soft-spoken man, with a beard, who dressed in corduroys, bit a pipe continually, and had another child, a daughter, as quiet as himself, and as devilish as the boy. "Mummy isn't angry with her little man," the woman said above her splashing. Silence when Norton was around being a sure sign he was into mischief, Phoebe looked across the hall where she saw him lifting a paint brush to a lambskin chair cover.

"Mummy," he called, "I'm being good. I'm painting now," just as Phoebe caught his raised arm. "Ouch!" he yelled. "Nasty Phoebe is hurting me." Then, "MUMMY!" as she tightened her fingers on the bristles he had slapped into her hand. A brown blob ran down her arm onto the floor.

Mrs. Jepson, wrapped in a towel, her skin rust-colored from scrubbing, tore in.

"With molasses," Phoebe sniffed. "I'll get some hot water. That should take it off." She did not want to watch how protectively the woman put arms about the child, crooning, "Baby, baby," and see him with his tongue sticking out as he peered over her shoulder.

Phoebe went into the pantry for bucket and detergent. A fat mouse knocked a box of oatmeal off the shelf, making another mess for her to clean up. How often had she planned on not coming to the Jepsons but somehow she always felt sorry for these people who seemed to create problems out of the simplest things; the mice, for instance. When she had first come to this remodeled farmhouse in the orchard, the place swarmed with mice.

"The Pied Piper led them here," Charles Jepson joked. The pantry was filled with an army gobbling its way into boxes, knocking things all over the floor, adding their own excretory contributions. At night, as the children went off to bed, furry bodies tumbled out of wall cracks to run up and down on them. "Sally, will you please stop poking that hole. Mummy doesn't think it looks pretty," Mrs. Jepson had said.

"I'm pushing the mousies' home," giggled Sally, as another chunk fell, widening the breach. She and Norton were one of a kind. Phoebe remembered how long the workmen, sent by the college, took to patch the plaster. "Lady," one complained, "everytime I fix it, I find it's been dug out. No mouse ever did that."

Finally it was Phoebe who bought two dozen mouse traps, baited them, then discovered that neither one of the Jepsons would remove the bodies. "Poor dears," sighed Mrs. Jepson.

Within the month, though, the horde had been reduced to a few field mice who strayed in from the orchard. At last the workmen went away, not that there weren't holes to be patched, but upon orders from some executive who figured the cost to the college. A neighbor presented a black kitten whom they named "Leonardo," but on the first moonlight night the serenades and the fights of the males for her favors proved the name incorrect.

Filling the bucket with hot water and pine-smelling detergent, Phoebe watched a gang of children race by the window in pursuit of "Lennie," and a ginger cat.

"Phoebe," Sally screamed at her, "hurry! The kittens are mating. We're all going to watch," as she ran to catch up with the others.

At ten-thirty, Mrs. Jepson reboiled the breakfast coffee for their ritual cup. Norton had been zippered into snowsuit, gone off to a neighbor's till luncheon. "Honestly, Phoebe," said Mrs. Jepson lighting a cigarette, "it must be a blessing to have peace and quiet around the house. I certainly envy you your life at times."

It was a fantasy she let the other woman indulge in, that the world without children ran smoothly, as if there were no illness, nor day-by-day accumulation of wear — still, all in all, Phoebe Butler rejoiced in the constant cycle of living.

"Yes, quieter," said Phoebe, seeing how the woman sprawled, her knees, her elbows, almost coming apart at the seams before her eyes. Not for one minute did she envy Mrs. Jepson, seeing the lines deepening around the corners of her face, the unnatural pallor, accentuated by the bronze hair dye she used to touch up her hair.

"Still, they have moments when they ease up," Mrs. Jepson said, looking out the window at the children standing on the edge of the maple grove, "when they listen and watch the world with innocent wonder. It's really a rich emotional experience to be a mother," she took a deep drag on the cigarette. "Oh, these taste vile," she said, dropping it with a hiss into her coffee cup. "Well, what's happening on Pleasant Street?"

"The purple finches came this morning," said Phoebe, "though they look more like they've been into raspberry or strawberry jam than grape." She swallowed the bitter coffee. "Spring is just around the corner when they come."

"Spring," snorted Mrs. Jepson. "What a joke! This orchard becomes a bog. Someday I think Charles and the children will sink out of sight in the mud, it's that deep." Drumming her fingers on the table, she said, "What are those children doing, sitting in the snow?"

"The cats are mating," Phoebe said.

"How sweet," said Mrs. Jepson. "That's one advantage of living here, you don't have to explain all that to them. You know, about the birds and bees. That darling Hegerstrom boy told Norton they had an unmarried rooster for Thanksgiving. Wasn't that charming?" She smiled at Phoebe.

There was so much work to be done that Phoebe had not been listening. Mrs. Jepson had a habit of bouncing from one topic to another without requiring answers; or she stayed on the endless theme of her children.

"Don't you think that's funny? A capon, an unmarried rooster?" she persisted.

Phoebe felt like telling her Wayne's remark, "Just tell 'em, don't explain 'em," but she did not say this. "A raccoon comes on our porch, peeks in the front parlor," she said, going to the world of nature for escape. "Every night this week he's been there, so we put bread out for him."

"Cute," said Mrs. Jepson, her face not friendly. "Do you still have your turtles?"

This was to joke her, Phoebe knew — the turtles, their slow ways a parody on her own staid manner. Her marriage, after forty, to Wayne Butler, a widower who waited till his two daughters set up housekeeping, and her renunciation till after her father's invalid dying, had ended a courtship that lasted over ten years. Anytime Mrs. Jepson found a cartoon about turtles, or long engagements, she never failed to call it to Phoebe's attention.

"Yes," said Phoebe, "but all they seem to do is sleep under their little bridge."

Mrs. Jepson laughed, "You're expecting chimes?"

The children thundered up the kitchen steps, flung open the door so that the floor boards shook. "We're hungry, feed us," Sally said to her mother.

"Darling," began Mrs. Jepson, ignoring the six other children, "haven't I taught you to say hello when I have people?"

"Where?" asked Sally, sticking her fingers in the sugar bowl, tipping it over.

Mrs. Jepson turned to Phoebe, "You see? You're like part of the family." She tapped her finger on the child's hand, "Naughty. I mean Phoebe, of course."

"Hello-Phoebe-we're-hungry-feed-us," said Sally.

Phoebe got up from the table to get a mop for the slush. The children surged into the pantry for a box of pretzels and a jar of peanut butter, moved as one body with them out of the house.

"Darling," said Mrs. Jepson, as the door slammed shut. "Damn," she sighed, "there are days I simply can't cope with them," and she went into the sewing room where she ran the machine full speed.

Phoebe had just finished mopping, sweeping the pantry after the mouse and children, was on her way upstairs when Mrs. Jepson called.

"Don't clean Mr., I mean Charles's studio. He's beginning a bird mobile with strings and cellophane. If a feather is misplaced," she paused, "well, you know his temper."

It was easy to see who Norton resembled at such times. Phoebe recognized another defeat. Never once had she been able to clean this house thoroughly. Constantly she was being thwarted by Mrs. Jepson's disorganization, or the children. She could spend her three hours, twice a week, simply picking up the accumulation of articles thrown in disorder from room to room. When she thought of what cleaning a house was like in her family, how every stick of furniture, walls, ceiling, were scrubbed of their winter's film, twice a week at the Jepsons' she was merely helping out. That made her feel better, not to say she cleaned but that she helped out. The time her age and arthritis interfered, she would leave this house first. She was scrubbing the tub when she heard the machine stop, the woman swearing in the sewing room. Probably has broken another needle, thought Phoebe, going in to help.

"I thought I would surprise Charles with new drapes, but now I've snapped another needle," said Mrs. Jepson, trying to get the wad of burlap untangled.

"He should be surprised," said Phoebe. "What color do you call that?"

"Chartreuse," Mrs. Jepson beamed. "It does have quite an effect, doesn't it?"

"Have to cut this free," said Phoebe. "You struck a pin in the hem." Instead of upstairs bedrooms, bathrooms, she spent the rest of the morning sewing the burlap drapes that they might be in place for a cocktail party later in the day.

When Wayne picked her up at the barn after twelve, she felt as if she had put in ten hours at the brush factory where she had worked as a girl.

"Norton?" her husband asked when he opened the car door, saw her face. She was so tired she nodded. His hand reached for hers. "How would you like me to fix a piping hot stack of buckwheats for lunch?" he asked. He could fix two meals, buckwheats, or scrambled eggs.

She smiled. "That would be lovely," and putting her head back on the seat, she thought again of the finches, of coming spring.

"Remember how we used to drive up to the hollow to listen to whippoorwills? You always told me they wouldn't sing till we got there."

"Just 'cause you saw purple finches, that don't mean the whippoorwills were fool enough to come," her husband said. "Radio reports another storm moving in from the west with six to eight inches of snow due." He pulled the car up to their house. "Go rest and I'll call you when it's ready." She noticed the turtle bowl looked empty with only the water, the stones, and the little bridge under which they slept.

Not only did Wayne fix buckwheat cakes and coffee, but he also did the dishes before he went back to the Worthington's, where he was one of the caretakers of the estate. "Now," he said, "you can spend the whole afternoon watching TV. See you at five."

Instead of turning on the set, she looked out at the feeder where she counted three male finches, two females. The sun had gone behind low clouds rolling in from the west. Even if it did snow, these lovely birds were a promise of spring; she had smelled the soft earth in the morning wind. The song of cats at night, though they wakened her, made her look forward to the litter of kittens. And the whole pond would come alive with more birds and creatures. Last year, beavers had made a dam farther up where the creek joined. Some boys had trapped one of them, threw the carcass with mangled paw back into the water, which then had washed below to where she found it. Now she walked over to the couch to lie down, still feeling very tired. The wind blew in the trees, rattled the window panes. She felt the muscles of her body tighten, then release with that feeling as though she were falling down a flight of stairs. The sight of Mrs. Jepson standing in the tub, the whole side of her body stained red appeared before her eyes in sleep, followed by confused dreams of swift black water closing over her, of singing children, and Wayne saying, "Whippoorwills cannot sing in the snow."

A slight thump woke her. She knew at once it was the raccoon, though her head was heavy with sleep. She heard it dragging its body across the porch to where she had a left a buckwheat cake. By the creature's slowness she knew there was something wrong. remembered the boys on the ridge that morning, how they had waited for her to go before tracking him down. Getting to her feet she went over to the window. It had fallen on its side, a young 'coon hardly larger than a cat, with a hole just below the neck on the left side where the bullet had entered. She saw it try to rise but fall back, this time the paws curved in, the eyes filmed over. The finches were a sign that spring was to come, when all things begin to live, except Wayne was right, winter would not leave gracefully and Vermont was still a state where to be natural meant sometimes dying, even though the full cycle of earth called for the beginning, not the end.

She went out to cover him with a rug till her husband returned to care for him. She recalled a sermon in church about Saint Francis and his friends the birds. The world was too large a place for her understanding; the wind, the purple finches could recall the whole soft living of spring, but boys killing could drive the sun from the sky, making the forest the dark place, such as the channel where the ice broke deep in swift-running water; and after filling a bowl with grain, she went outside to the feeder, while the finches sat chirping from the lilac bush till once again she was at a safe distance.